being written

being written

a novel

WILLIAM CONESCU

HARPER 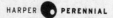 PERENNIAL

NEW YORK • LONDON • TORONTO • SYDNEY • NEW DELHI • AUCKLAND

HARPER ● PERENNIAL

P.S.™ is a trademark of HarperCollins Publishers.

HarperCollins books may be purchased for educational, business, or sales promotional use. For information please write: Special Markets Department, HarperCollins Publishers, 10 East 53rd Street, New York, NY 10022.

FIRST EDITION

Designed by Laura Kaeppel

Library of Congress Cataloging-in-Publication Data is available upon request.

ISBN 978-0-06-145134-8

08 09 10 11 12   OV/RRD   10 9 8 7 6 5 4 3 2 1

With love to
Mom, Dad, Allison, Nancy,
and Granny

being written

ELL, WHAT ELSE is a girl to do?" she says to the bartender with a prolonged giggle. And it's not the question that draws your attention to the young woman sitting alone
at the bar, or the laughter, which distinctly lacks sincerity, but
that scratching sound. The scratching of a pencil. It's not your
pencil because you've put it down. And the bartender is just listening to the woman, not writing anything. There's not another
soul in the bar. It's just as empty as it was when you settled into
one of the pinewood booths half an hour ago. But the scratching . . . it's coming from her corner of the bar. Did it just start,
or did you somehow fail to notice it when you first arrived?
Without thinking, you walk toward the bar, toward her and the
sound, and yes, the scratching grows louder. It's centered on
her, remains with her when the bartender steps away, hangs
in the air around her as she silently contemplates her martini

glass. There's no question about it. That's the scratching of the author's pencil. She's being written.

"Can I help you, sir?" the bartender asks.

You turn from the woman to face him. How long have you been standing here, listening? You look back at the woman's tangle of short, black curls, then at him. You'd order a drink, but you have a nearly full pint of beer back at your table. They can see it from here. Still, you have to explain yourself.

"Um . . ."

Often an "um" will naturally lead to a statement, but you can think of nothing to say. The scratching is quite distracting. The woman turns to look at you, and now they're both staring, waiting, and you can feel your face turning red, your ears, your neck. Why can't you just say something? You're finally in a book again. You've waited three years for another chance. You could have a real line of dialogue this time if you would just open your mouth. Just speak. Just say—

"Can I please borrow a pencil?" Your eyes move from one of them to the other, then rest on the woman.

"Sure," she says before the bartender can respond. She grabs a large, black macramé bag from the stool beside her and starts fishing through it.

"Mine broke," you lie. "Sorry."

"No problem," she says, her head still buried in the bag. She looks to be about five years younger than you, somewhere in her midtwenties, with skin especially pale against her dark hair and short black dress. From the booth, her dress looked kind of elegant, but up close you can see that it's made of knit cotton and is covered in lint. "Here we go," she declares at last, offering you a pen and an impish smile.

"Thank you," you say, waiting for further inspiration. But none comes, so you return to your booth.

What is it about her that has drawn the author's attention? How far along is this book, you wonder, and how are you going to get a footing in it? Being Man-Who-Borrows-Pen is little better than being some nondescript, silent body having a drink in the background. If you want to work your way into this story, you've got to do more. Now think.

A minute passes. Then two. But your next move is hard to figure out. Having a special skill doesn't necessarily mean a person's going to be able to make the best use of it. Like, they say some people can smell the rain coming, but that's only going to be helpful for someone who becomes a farmer or mountain climber or something. Twins sometimes claim to have a psychic bond, but that's bound to get annoying unless they're saving each other's lives or finding each other's lost car keys. And when you discovered, back at the age of twenty-one, that your entire world is simply the imagination of an author and that you have the unusual ability to hear when the author happens to be writing about someone nearby . . . well, what the hell were you supposed to do with that? It's rather disheartening. Like the grown-up equivalent of finding out there's no Santa Claus. Or worse. Really, much worse. Because if you're just here to fill out the landscape and provide the world with an infrastructure so that other people's lives can be written, then your own life can feel kind of pointless. Yet when the morning comes, you still have to wake up, go to work, pay the bills, fill the time. It was only after you'd passed in and out of a few books that you started to wonder if you could serve some greater purpose on the page.

So you read up. You read lots and lots of novels to figure out what it might take to get a decent part, maybe even be a protagonist one day. But you don't have limitless frequent flier miles or a knack for defusing bombs or charming snakes. You don't have a son who can't get picked for the baseball team, a high-paying job that doesn't interfere with your busy schedule, a computer with access to the FBI database, or friends who owe you favors scattered about the globe. You weren't molested as a child, didn't have to overcome enormous obstacles only to face even greater ones. You don't have a dark past, a bright future, a pure heart, a great mind, a chiseled jaw, a sultry lover, or a gun. Why would you expect the author to focus on you?

So you've been working on it. You were on the track team at Boston University, so you keep it up, running a few days a week at the gym or outside if it's not too cold. You could outrun an attacker, run five miles in thirty minutes to deliver a secret antidote. You took karate classes for a while and made it up to a green belt. You had the LASIK surgery—didn't want glasses to become your Achilles' heel. You've been thinking about buying a gun and going to a shooting range, but you haven't had the time yet. And though you can take a class to learn to shoot or master karate or overcome a speech impediment, you cannot take a course in charisma. So coming up with something to say to this woman—who's rather pretty and probably out of your league—is not that easy.

"In the mood for a little company?"

She's standing beside your booth holding a pink martini. You didn't even see her walk up.

"My name's Delia Benson," she continues, sitting down across from you with a pleasant, rhetorical "May I?"

"Daniel Fischer," you say, sliding your pencil off the table. It's supposed to be broken; you crack the tip on the bench beside you.

"So, Daniel," she says, "I practically live at Lilly's, but I don't think I've seen you here before."

You look up and let your eyes survey the oil paintings interspersed among neon beer signs. "No," you say. "I was just having dinner over in Porter Square with . . ." You are about to bore yourself, so you let the words trail off, hoping you both can ignore the false start.

"Yes, I see. And dinner went so well that you hurried down the block afterward to have a drink in peace. Bad date?" she asks, raising one dark eyebrow. There is something feline about her movements. She rests her arms flat on the table and maintains the inquisitive expression until you blush.

"No, parents," you explain. "They were passing through Boston on their way back from Atlantic City, and they had to tell me about every bet made at every casino."

"I can see how that might require lubrication," she says.

You smile and take a sip of beer to fill the pause, but then you swallow wrong and start to choke. So you hold your breath for a few seconds, but you can feel your face turning red as the foam starts to move back up. And she's watching you, her brow slightly crinkled, and you will the beer not to shoot out of your nose. Not now. But it's close, and you're going to need to breathe again soon, and this moment is not helping move the conversation along. So, carefully, you cough a few drops into your hand—just drops, not ounces, nothing conspicuous—and the danger passes.

"Are you okay?" she asks.

You nod. You are not making a stellar impression. Not a particularly smooth entrance onto the page.

"Are you sure? Your ears turned red."

"Yes," you say. "I'm fine. They just do that sometimes." Man-Whose-Ears-Turn-Red-Sometimes. You shouldn't be allowed to speak.

"So you're a writer?"

The question startles you before you register her quick glance at the notebook in front of you. "No," you tell her, hurriedly closing it and pushing it aside. "No, this is nothing. I work in marketing."

"I didn't ask what you do for a living. If you're like ninety-nine percent of the people in the world, what you do to pay the bills is meaningless. Wouldn't it be nice if we could just take care of ourselves? Just grow our own food—or kill it, build a house, and call it a day?"

"Oh, yeah," you say. "Sure."

"Not that I could actually build a house, but I'm sure I could learn to garden. They say it's relaxing. . . . I could help grow your food, and you could build my house. Of course, that's the beginning of society again. Only a few steps from there to Wal-Mart and consulting firms."

"I actually work at a consulting firm."

"And why wouldn't you?" she says with a light chuckle.

The bar door creaks open behind you, and she throws a glance over your head, then takes a long sip of her drink. "Now," she says, and she rests a hand on top of yours, "tell me what you're writing. Is it a novel?"

You're not sure what to say at first—your notebook is filled with useless scribbles about how to sell computer processors and financial services—so you settle on a definite "Sort of."

"Well, I don't want to put words in your mouth."

"No, it is," you lie. "It's a novel."

"That's very exciting," she says. "I love novels. What's it about?"

You give yourself a second to think. Could the author be playing with you? "I haven't quite figured it out yet," you tell her.

"Well, what's happened so far?"

"Not much. There's this guy. He's in his thirties."

"And?"

You sip your beer cautiously, then shrug. "Like I said, I really just started. Nothing interesting has happened yet."

"That's half the fun, isn't it? You could do anything to him. Put him in the path of danger, send him on a quest. He could become a heroin addict, maybe. I've known two. It's quite terrible."

"Well," you say, "I guess. Or something good could always happen to him."

"Of course," she says. "Anything at all."

You feel yourself begin to smile. "There is something a little freeing about not knowing where you're headed."

"Exactly. And if you don't like the character or what he does, you can always start over, invent someone exciting. They're only words. You can make more."

"No," you tell her. This feels like a test of some sort. "No, I'm going to stick with him."

"Well, good. Go for it," she says in exactly the same enthusiastic tone she used when suggesting you abandon the project. "You must have started this way for a reason. It'll work itself out." Now Delia thrusts her glass high in the air, splashing a good bit of the pink cocktail onto her fingers. "Here's to the next Great American Novel," she says.

"I hope so," you say, clinking your glass to hers.

It might just be the beer—and the half a bottle of wine you had at dinner—but you're starting to feel a little more confident, even somewhat excited. After all, here you are talking to a charming woman in an empty bar. The pencil is still scratching. If the author didn't intend for you two to meet, at least the conversation has been interesting enough to be recorded. You just need to stay calm. Something might come of this.

"YOU'LL HAVE TO excuse the mess."

Delia's apartment is many levels beyond "mess." She must have given up some time ago. Walls, furniture, and floors alike are all covered in a bright patchwork of pictures, postcards, dishes, books, and clothes—some worn and cast aside, others apparently clean, abandoned in small piles. A piano with chipping paint sits right inside the front door, surrounded by stacks of sheet music, a mound of beach towels, and a dying ficus tree. In the middle of the apartment, beside a burgundy sofa, a large calico cat rests on a green checked loveseat—or rather, on a pair of stockings, on a magazine, on a Mexican afghan, on the loveseat.

"Myra!" Delia says to the cat, who raises her eyes but not her bulk in response. "I named her for *Myra Breckinridge*. Gore Vidal? Have you read it? "

You shake your head.

"I'll have to find it and lend it to you."

As she moves to the kitchen, you marvel that she could find anything in this wreckage, but as if to disprove your thoughts, she returns almost immediately with two glasses and a bottle of wine. "Tucked away for a rainy day."

"Why is it such a rainy day?" you ask.

But she ignores the question, depositing the two glasses on the coffee table and turning to you with the wine bottle and corkscrew. "Would you?" she says, and she hands them to you before busying herself with a pile of CDs on the floor.

She let you hold every door for her—at the bar, your car, the gate in front of her house. She lives a few minutes away from Lilly's on the top floor of a three-family house near Davis Square in Somerville. When you parked across the street, she even waited for you to open the car door for her. Not that you mind. It's nice to participate.

The scratching sound has followed you to the apartment, but now Ella Fitzgerald obscures it with a fast-paced scat through the speakers. The music is comforting, and when you look up from the wine, you find Delia standing beside you. You tentatively offer her a glass, nervous somehow, as if you're responsible for the vintage. She takes a small sip and instantly pronounces it "de*li*cious."

It's a little heavy, actually. A cheap merlot. But you take a couple of substantial gulps before settling into the thin cushions of the sofa. "So, you were having a rainy day—"

"Oh, God, yes. Going to Lilly's with my friends is usually guaranteed to put me in a good mood. But no one could meet me tonight, and it's awful to be trapped alone in your apartment with a bad mood, don't you think? Especially at night. Problems grow, become so unwieldy." Delia sips her wine again, then settles into the opposite corner of the sofa.

"What problems?" you ask cautiously. Maybe you're about to find out why she gets a book written about her. Maybe that's why you're in the book, to give her this opportunity to articulate her problems.

"Oh, I don't know," she says. "I'm not myself tonight. Well, I guess this is a part of me, but not the me I'm proud to call me. Does that make sense?"

Her eyes are so dark and her lips so pert, so sensual.

"Sometimes I feel like I spend half of my time negotiating the various me's—me, myself, and I. If only there were just three! You have to be someone different for everyone you know, everything you do. It's hard to just be yourself. Be real." Delia sets her glass down on the coffee table and looks you in the eyes. "I think it's wonderful that you're a writer. I'm a singer. That's the real me. I should be following in Ella's footsteps, but it's so easy to lose track, you know?" Her hand reaches over to touch your cheek, and the chill of her fingers surprises you. "Would you mind massaging my neck for a minute?" she asks, her voice retaining some of the sadness of her speech. "Just a quick rub," she says, turning away from you. "To get the knots out."

The request unsettles you, though of course, the prospect of making love to this woman did enter your mind when you left the bar with her. It's been a few months. Five—no, six, actually. Mechanically, you reach over to set your wineglass on the table beside hers, but your hands are unsteady and you splash wine onto your fingers. So now where are you going to wipe them off? You glance around for a napkin, then Delia pulls your hand toward her and licks the drops from your fingertips.

When she releases your hand, you take a deep breath, then shift, and cautiously begin to rub her shoulders. Her skin is cool, and her curls smell like some flowery shampoo, and you are tentative in your movements until she sighs, "Mmm, right there," and you knead the spot with your thumbs. The massage continues through one song and then another before Delia turns and looks you in the eye and says, "I wish we could just be naked."

The words sound a little forced, almost scripted, but a moment later she's leaning forward and kissing you, her cold hand gripping the back of your neck. Her lips are sticky with lipstick and wine and pink cocktails, and her breath is warm and sweet. With Ella belting out "Nice Work If You Can Get It," Delia pushes you backward onto the sofa. Your arms wrap around her and hold the small of her back, and she reaches down with one hand and pulls your shirttail out of your pants.

Then the song changes, and during the pause, you can hear the pencil scratching in the background, can feel the author's scrutiny. You try to lean up to kiss her neck, but twice your nose bumps into her chin, and her hair keeps falling into your mouth. You shudder at the chill of her fingers on your stomach, and you know you need to relax. When Delia pulls away for a second and asks if everything's okay, you make yourself smile. You say, "Sure." She says, "Good."

Bodies shift. Dress, shirt, and pants are shed. Ella launches into "A Foggy Day," and you wonder what you look like to the author as you brace yourself awkwardly above Delia's small frame. This is not the kind of part you've ever pictured yourself playing. Not that it's a bad part, but you always imagined it would be more of an action sequence that would ease you into a book: a hostage situation, bank robbery, fire, car chase. Sex is something you're happy to do off the page, in the dark, without an audience.

Delia slides her hand beneath the waistband of your boxers. "Is it that she's watching?" she asks.

What?

Delia glances over at the cat, who stares at the two of you with a look of profound boredom.

No, you say, no, you're fine—but then you excuse yourself to go to the bathroom.

Hair a bit disheveled, forehead moist with sweat. Still, in the dim light, your freckles are less pronounced, your hair isn't so red, and the little lines around your eyes are almost invisible. You're not the best-looking man on the planet, but at thirty-one, you still have a vaguely youthful appearance. You could pass for . . . well, twenty-nine, maybe. But no one mistakes you for being older, anyway, and the women who always seem to be chatting outside your office have called you handsome more than once. In a maternal tone, but they seem sincere.

Through the cracked door of the bathroom, the song

changes and again you can hear the pencil scratching in the next room. Why is this so difficult? You should enjoy the time you have on the page. It's not often that you cross paths with a book being written, and the only other time you've had a part of any consequence, you were too busy thinking you were going to be killed to appreciate what was happening. Right now, you get to make love to a beautiful woman in a book. That's what the author wants to show people: you, in there, with Delia. "It's kind of hot," you whisper. And now the stirring you felt when she licked your fingers returns, and you can feel your heart pounding.

You return to the living room a transformed man, pulling Delia up into your embrace and forcing a deep kiss upon her. She relinquishes herself to you, you abandon the last of your clothes, and the cat closes her eyes as you slip inside Delia. At first, she grips your waist and breathes heavily, but once you achieve a certain momentum, she drifts into silence, her lips parted slightly, her eyes unfocused. You look beyond Delia and strain to make out the scratching behind the music. You have never felt such intense desire, such exhilaration. You imagine yourself standing apart, silently watching the scene, and this image, coupled with a long, whispered sigh from Delia, carries you through to a powerful climax.

In the calm that follows, Delia leads you to her bedroom, where she immediately curls into a ball beneath the cotton sheets. You climb into the bed beside her, and she pulls your arm around her waist. After a minute, the cat jumps onto the foot of the bed and circles a few times before curling up between your legs. You're still picturing your lovemaking as it must have appeared. You listen for the author's pencil but can hear nothing but Delia's slow breathing, the muffled calls of Ella in the next room, and the motorized purr of the cat. You wonder if the noise will keep you awake. You wonder what the next day will bring. You remember the poor showing you made earlier in the evening, but then the rush of your closing performance returns as all sound begins to fade.

YOU ARE SHOCKED back to consciousness by the slam of a door. You're in a strange bed, alone. As your eyes adjust to the light pouring in through the thin drapes and you try to make out a scratching in the air, a tall figure comes into view: a man in his early twenties with golden-brown hair down to his shoulders. He's wearing a plaid shirt, a thin gold chain around his neck, and a wide grin.

"Good morning," he says, his voice surprisingly deep-pitched for his boyish face. He looks like an overgrown teenager—easily six-three, six-four—with big features, a big square jaw and big blue eyes, extra-long fingers, extra-long neck, and when he reaches down to offer you an enormous hand, his arm seems to extend for miles. You use one hand to pull up the sheets and the other to greet him, but your hand is still asleep and it's crushed in his tight grip. "I see we've been busy," he says, still grinning. "I'm Graham."

"Daniel," you manage to say, your voice hoarse.

"How can you be so energetic?" shouts a woman from out-side the door. *Delia*, you remember. That's her name. She slips in behind Graham wearing a light pink bathrobe and holding a coffee mug, and when he jerks her forward and begins to kiss her, she shoves him away. "I haven't even brushed my teeth yet," she mutters. "And neither have *you*." She stares down at the floor for a moment before turning her heavy eyes to face you. "Have you two met?" she asks.

"We haven't shot the shit much or compared notes," Graham

announces in a disturbingly cheerful tone, "but we've covered first names. This is something, Delia."

"Isn't it?" she says. "So how was last night? Vile as usual?"

"It's never vile," he says. "It was three hundred fifty dollars, and nearly effortless."

"Yes, I've heard the speech." Delia disappears for a moment, then returns with your clothing from the living room. "Sorry to get you up so early," she says, tossing the wrinkled mound onto the corner of the bed.

"What time is it?" you ask.

"Six something."

"Well, that's good, actually. I have to go home and change."

"Want to borrow something of mine?" Graham suggests. "Something *else?*"

"Graham!"

"Sweetheart, I couldn't resist. I'm only playing."

No one has anything to say for a minute, and you want to dress and leave as quickly as possible, but Graham doesn't move. Doesn't look like he has any plan to move. He's planted beside the bed, the remnant of a smile lingering. Delia leans against the dresser and sips her coffee.

You clear your throat. "Well," you say to the footboard, "I guess I'll just get dressed and get out of your way."

"No hurry," Graham replies.

"Just let him get dressed, Graham!" She's a little less charming this morning.

"I'm not stopping him," he says, and then turns toward you. "No need to be shy on my account."

"For Christ's sake," she says, storming into the living room.

Graham turns to follow but pauses in the doorway. "Better see what's eating the little woman," he says with a wink. "Seriously, if you need anything, mine is the second closet, the one in the corner there." And finally he goes, closing the door behind him.

What was that? She didn't act like a woman cheating on her husband or boyfriend or whatever, and Graham didn't seem angry, not exactly. As you pull on your pants, you spot a large pair of tennis shoes on the floor in the corner. How did you not realize there was someone else living here? You did notice last night that the shaving cream in the bathroom was a man's brand, but you didn't think much of it.

So what does this make you? Man-Delia-Screwed-Once? That doesn't seem fair. "Please," you whisper to the air around you, "let me stay in this story. I'll do anything you want. Just let me know, give me a sign or something." Of course there's no response. There's never a response. Just you buttoning your shirt in some other man's bedroom about to be shuffled off the page. "*Please,*" you say again, a little louder.

When you step out into the living room, Delia is sitting quietly with Graham on the sofa. She seems calm now. Two mugs sit on the coffee table in front of them. "Sorry for the rude awakening," she says.

"Don't worry about all this," he tells you.

What is that supposed to mean?

"Well," you say, "it was good to meet you both." And you know that sounds stupid, but what's the right thing to say?

Then, as you pass the sofa on the way to the door, Delia extends an arm and gently caresses your waist, sending a charge through your body that starts with anger and ends with sadness. You stand in front of the door for a moment, reluctant to reach for the knob but wary of turning back to face them. This can't be it for you.

"Bye," Delia calls after you.

"Bye," you say, glancing back. Graham waves. Delia watches you, her face without expression.

You open the door. You walk out.

But the scratching stays behind.

Delia

DELIA IS WEARING the kind of outfit that her father once said reminded him of a child playing dress-up in her parents' closet: black patent leather boots, gray silk shirt and red Chanel scarf over an ancient T-shirt, wool pants washed a few dozen times too many, and a pinstripe blazer manufactured three decades ago for men. Her unnaturally black curls stand up in all directions. Pale skin. Little makeup, save for the Kewpie-doll red lips, which don't even part into a half-smile when the cries of the tone-deaf singer begin echoing through the underground T station at Davis Square.

From her bench against the back wall, Delia surveys the crowd of swarming commuters and spots Broadway Lady near the far escalator. She's wearing a new wig, pink. But that doesn't help. Usually, the old woman's appearance is a good omen for the day. Delia will sometimes call Graham on her cell phone if there's time. The woman can't sing two consecutive notes correctly and generally mumbles the lyrics, so playing Name That Tune can be surprisingly difficult. But this morning, Delia is distracted by thoughts of Graham and a man named Daniel, whose last name she can't recall.

She still can't believe she went through with it. But she had to get through to Graham somehow. They couldn't have the same argument for the fiftieth time—the argument could argue itself by now. When he first mentioned this whole thing a few months ago, he caught her completely off guard. And there was no reasoning with him. So when she saw Daniel . . . The memory of Daniel's body against hers is surprisingly vivid, and she can feel the color rise to her face. If Graham had just listened to her, been a little realistic, she wouldn't have had to—

Saved by the train. Delia pushes herself through the mob, at once detesting each person for his presence and envying each for his thoughts. Any thoughts but these. She braces herself as the train jerks away from the station. Soon, she thinks. Soon she will switch into her work self and think entirely different thoughts, thoughts which have nothing to do with Graham or their relationship or his little show this morning—or hers last night. . . . But then it's also disturbing to realize how easily she can make the transformation from life and infidelity to acknowledgment letters and fundraising goals, catered lunch-meetings and lupus.

Three years have passed since Delia started working at the McKlein Lupus Foundation, though it was supposed to be a temporary thing. She had just had a large cyst removed from one of her ovaries, and while it wasn't a dangerous procedure, the doctor thought she shouldn't be on her feet all night waitressing. A friend of her father's was on the foundation's board at the time; he suggested the foundation hire her to help out with the fiscal year end. It was all very informal. She didn't even have to fill out an application. Then the ovary healed, the fiscal year ended, and instead of going back to the restaurant, Delia stayed. They needed help with the annual fund, and she kept delaying the move to New York. And she figured at least she was doing something arguably good for the world.

How far removed she feels from the *good* her foundation does. Certainly lupus is a debilitating disease and of course the world needs a cure. But the foundation serves as a middleman between the people and organizations that make gifts and the researchers and caregivers that receive grants. It's a necessary function, like her father's firm, which does import-export work, but how fulfilling can that role ever be? At least once a week, she suffers an attack of guilt for not investing emotionally in her work—or even in the fight against lupus—but the path between what she does and what good might result from it is so long and circuitous that it feels like she could just as easily be selling mail-order cosmetics or working as an accountant's assistant. Maybe the other people at the foundation have to feign enthusiasm, too. She can't even talk about the job in front of Graham. That look he gets in his eyes . . .

When the train reaches Kendall Square, Delia realizes she has fought off the metamorphosis too successfully, and she instinctively pulls out her phone to call Monty. But then she stops herself. He wouldn't skip work. Nor would she. And what would she even say to him? Though she's known Monty forever, she wouldn't dream of telling him about last night. No. Best to stop off at the Methodist Home.

The Methodist Home for the Aging is on Second Street two blocks north of Delia's office, and with a mixture of anticipation and shame, she makes a quick survey of the street before hurrying through the glass doors. The air smells of sickness and fake flowers. The bright fluorescent lights reflect off the white linoleum floor, and Delia leaves her sunglasses on until she passes the waiting area with its sad, vinyl furniture and sad, expectant faces.

At the reception desk, a heavy woman with poorly dyed blond curls winks at Delia. "Well, hello, darling," she says. "You come by to sing for us again?"

"Well, I wondered if you might have some time around lunch."

The receptionist pores over a clipboard, her head floating somewhere between a nod and a slow stretch, before the movement resolves itself into a shake of the head coupled with an exaggerated frown. "Not today, honey. Looks like we have a visit from the church choir at twelve and then the arts and crafts people coming right after."

"Oh, well . . ."

"Want to come by on Tuesday? You know Mr. Demarco misses you."

Delia smiles, promises to return the following week, then hurries across the street into the coffee shop. Her visits to the Methodist Home began about two years ago, when one of her aunts moved there, and although the aunt soon moved to her daughter's house in New Hampshire, Delia continued to visit the home every few weeks. She would like to believe she cares for her aunt's one-time friends, but in truth, they tend to blend together in her mind. It's their quiet, uncritical applause that continues to draw her back.

Delia settles into a back table at the coffee shop and picks the cranberries out of her muffin, willing the hour hand on her watch not to strike nine. The man at the table beside her is writing furiously in a journal, and Delia's mind returns to Daniel. Before last night, she hadn't been with another man in six years—since she was *twenty*. And good Lord, what does she even know about this guy? He's a writer. Working on a novel. There was something about him, a pent-up urgency. He was quite attentive—not in the pretentious way that Natalie, Monty's girlfriend, claims every experience is "fruit" for her "work," but in a jumbled, more earnest way. It's a shame Delia had to be a little unkind to him in the end.

She wonders if she'll ever walk into Cambridge Books and see Daniel's face blown up on one of those giant posters. *I never would have thought to write about heroin addicts if it weren't for this girl I met. . . .* The thought sends a shiver through her entire body. But of course, normal people never find commercial success. He probably won't even get published. It's only the stockbroker–turned–romance novelist who makes it big these days. Even Natalie said so, though she'd probably deny it now that she's moving up the publishing ladder. Big New York job. Fawning over books about girls who work at a soup kitchen for half an hour and then discover God. Those with real talent don't work in publishing and don't get contracts. They have to work at coffee shops or divert their talent to make money in commercial pursuits. Or in nonprofits, as the case may be.

"Hi, Delia."

Delia looks up, conscious of the cranberry skin stuck between her teeth. It's Jennifer, that horror from the foundation. Delia smiles with her lips closed.

"Slow start this morning?" Jennifer got her muffin to go. Does that make her superior? Apparently so.

"Actually, I was running early, so I thought I'd treat my-self to breakfast."

"I wish I could," Jennifer says, her starched, spherical hair barely moving in spite of several enthusiastic bobs of the head. "We were there until eight last night working on the big Mentrek Labs proposal."

Congratulations, Delia would like to say. You care the most. But she just smiles again, and Jennifer leaves. Part of the transformation involves smiling at people she hates. It's about time to begin the day.

Graham

THE SHEET MUSIC in front of Graham is blank save for a few chords he's written in, but he's playing Brahms's Intermezzo in A Minor now. Not a particularly difficult piece for an experienced pianist, but Graham tears through it in double time. It was one of his early recital pieces, and he plays it as others might take a walk without noticing the trees or people around them, to relax his body while he meditates on nonmusical thoughts.

Did he really force her to bring a man home—and into their bed? Does that even make sense? How did he end up taking responsibility for that? Graham's fingers attack the keyboard, and he tries not to picture it. In the bed. Or in the shower. Or in the living room—there are lots of places not to picture things. So, fine. What's done is done. Now he'll just get a job of some sort. That's what normal people do, as

Delia is so fond of saying. They work. You don't have to love it, Monty said last time. And the time before. Just something to pay the bills.

But doing something awful for forty hours a week is not okay, Graham thinks. He'll die. How do people do it? They must like it on some level. Delia's probably at her office by now, twisting arms and coercing old people to give money. Graham has six hundred dollars to his name. He paid Delia back for May's rent, but June is going to come eventually. A wave of tension rushes to his neck, and his fingers instinctively drift into ragtime, as if the bouncing melody holds the solution to all problems. And since he's started to confuse "Maple Leaf Rag" and "The Entertainer," the activity does provide a distraction, until one of the pieces—or both or some combination—comes to an abrupt end.

The quiet startles him, and he jumps up and walks through the apartment in search of a stray sock to pick up or a piece of bread he should eat. The bread is stale, and of course, none of the stray socks are his. Myra is sleeping under Delia's abandoned bath towel, and when Graham throws a foam ball against the mound, the towel merely sighs. The cat probably wishes he'd leave the apartment, too. "A dog would be grateful to have me," he tells her. Now she doesn't even sigh. If they'd broken up this morning, Delia would have taken Myra. And the furniture, dishes, all that crap. In fact, in the five years they've lived together—hell, ever since he left Texas—he's managed to live a very lightweight existence. All he *needs* he could probably carry down the stairs in one load—except for the piano.

This interferes with Graham's theory of his own portability, and as he doesn't like being contradicted, even by himself, he reaches for a cigarette. His rolling papers are in a drawer of the coffee table, but he takes a light out of his pocket instead. The hand-rolled cigarettes have long been a habit, something he associates with his personality, like the long hair and the plaid shirts and the thin gold chain he wears, but Graham has been finding the unfiltered cigarettes rather harsh of late and has been smoking lights in private. The first puff is soothing, and Graham settles into the sofa. He isn't inspired to work on his sonata, and it seems trite to forage through sheet music to dig up pieces he mastered years ago. Television is always depressing. So Graham calls Jon.

No answer at the apartment, but Jon answers his cell phone after several rings. He's at the gym, finishing up in the locker room. "Flawless timing," he tells Graham. "I even have my pants on." They agree to meet at the Silent Owl in thirty minutes.

Graham wonders what he'll do with the next hour, since Jon will never be there in thirty minutes. Jon likes to tell people that he developed his punctuality problem in the womb and that he hasn't yet offended anyone so much as his mother, who didn't go into labor until almost her tenth month. Somehow the line still makes Graham smile, but how many times has he heard it now?

Though his hair is still wet from the first shower, Graham figures he might as well take another. He was too distracted earlier. It was hard to concentrate on rinsing the shampoo all the way down to the roots, covering every inch of his body with the washcloth, building up a good lather. The second shower is much more satisfying, and for a few minutes, it feels as if the past twelve hours have been washed away, too. He puts on another fresh T-shirt and pair of boxers, takes his time selecting an overshirt. If the trains are running without delays, he'll probably still beat Jon.

The Silent Owl is a lounge by night and coffeehouse by day, but mostly Graham thinks of it as a mausoleum for patterned fabrics. Sofas are carefully selected off the side of the road and installed in place of even more tattered furniture or, more often, in addition to the existing seats, now requiring new arrangements designed to obstruct movement. Once a customer manages to maneuver his way to a seat, it is best for all parties if he remains seated for the duration of his stay. The wispy waitresses slither through the maze of clunky furniture with surprising ease, even at night when the room is so dimly lit that Graham can hardly make out the faces of people coming or going. The Silent Owl at night is a good place to disappear.

"Sorry I'm late," Jon calls from the front door. In spite of the mild chill that will remain in Boston for at least a few more weeks, Jon is wearing just a sleeveless navy shirt and khaki pants. His manufactured tan shows off the definition in his arms, and his dirty-blond hair is in its usual state of cultivated dishevelment. As always, Jon looks striking, and his loud entrance attracts both hungry and annoyed glances from the other coffee drinkers. But he's used to the attention, Graham knows. Jon has thirteen years on Graham, and ten on Delia, but people never guess it.

"You wouldn't believe what I saw in the locker room," Jon says, dropping into the gold paisley chair across from Graham.

"I probably would."

"Two fifteen-year-old boys are in the sauna, and they're just going at it. Right there. I mean, honestly, they're practically children!"

"They *are* children."

"But I mean they were *all over* each other. They nearly imploded when I walked in on them, but I just turned around.

Told them to have fun. I mean, they should. You're only young once. Or twice. Wish I'd been so bold at fifteen."

"I always imagined you as the elementary school heartthrob, seducing little boys in the sandbox."

"Are you kidding? I was obsessed with purity. God, was I righteous. I went on a camping trip with the Cub Scouts and made them burn up their *Playboy* in the campfire. Said I'd tell the Scout leader or whatever he was. First time I saw a picture of a naked woman. Ooo. I learned a little something on that trip, and it wasn't how to tie a square knot."

Jon can talk for hours. He tends bar three nights a week at a moderately seedy South End gay bar, and there seems to be no end to the string of stories the bar provides. They must be exaggerations, could be lies, but it doesn't matter. Graham is relieved to lose himself in Jon's detailed summary of the night before. "I tell you," Jon sighs, having reached the finale, "it was a troll night for sure. You could've made a fortune." The conclusion of the story puts Graham back in sour spirits, and he sucks down the last of his Bloody Mary. "Sorry," Jon mumbles.

Graham shrugs. "That's all right. You're not the only one who thinks I've been stupid."

"Honey, can you blame her?"

Graham pulls out his rolling paper and tobacco and starts rolling a cigarette on the orange crate that serves as their coffee table. "She brought a man home last night," he says without lifting his gaze. "To illustrate her point."

"Oh . . ."

Then Graham lights his cigarette, and Jon flags a passing waitress. "Another Mary for him and—make it two," Jon tells her. "I'm sorry, honey. Look at me blathering on with my tales of old men and teenage erotica."

Graham relates his morning encounter and the brief conversation he had with Delia afterward. "So I said fine, I'll stop—but you have to admit, it's not the same thing as picking someone up at a bar."

"No," Jon says, "but it's not totally unrelated."

"But with me, there's no desire involved, no kissing—no mouth. And I was doing it with *guys*—who were usually pretty heinous, by the way. It's not like I was going to leave her for a *guy*."

"Yes, we know," Jon says, "but the bottom line is that her boyfriend is fucking other people. That can't feel good."

"Like, two or three times a month," Graham says. "And I told her, it doesn't feel good to me when she goes to that massage guy she adores. He spends an hour with his hands all over her. And he has to care. Me, I'm in and out. And I barely touch some of these guys."

"But you understand—"

"*Yes*, I understand." The waitress arrives with their drinks, and Graham happily dives into his. Jon, too. They've been through all this before. Hell, Jon's the one who told Graham how common it was for straight guys to do it for pay. Not that he was advocating it as a profession, but still.

"And," Jon says—he's not going to let this die—"Giorgio the masseur is not going to give her, or *you*, herpes or HIV—"

"You know how careful I am."

"—and he's not going to chop off her head and store it in his freezer. No matter how careful a person is, it's not like Jeffrey Dahmer wore a special crazy-badge to identify himself. 'Room for one more head in the freezer.'"

"Right back at you," Graham says. Even if half the stories are lies, Jon is still the most promiscuous person Graham knows.

"I am a shadow of my former slutty self," Jon insists with a dramatic swig of his drink. "Plus, I have strict rules about where I'll go. We do it in the sauna like civilized people, or we go back to my place where I know what's in the fridge."

"Freezer."

Jon sighs. "Honestly, I have no idea what's in my freezer."

Graham goes through two more cigarettes before they leave, and the conversation moves mercifully away from him and back to more comfortable topics like Gershwin and the divorce rates of pop stars and the future of Jon's sideburns, and at the end of the visit, when Graham gives Jon a hug, Jon says, "I'm glad this is over, because you two have been through too much together to throw it away over something stupid like this. You're *Delia and Graham*, for God's sake!"

"I know, I know," he says. "We'll be fine. I'll go sell shit, or smile at people and bring them food—like a 'normal person.'"

"You're a clever boy. I'm sure you can come up with a fine source of gainful employment. And please, you have to admit this was not your most brilliant plan. It'll have to be a relief to stop."

Graham holds the door for Jon as they walk outside, and yes, he thinks, it probably will be something of a relief. He's only been doing it for three months, but already he's been seeing an unattractive side of himself. And yet, in the past month, he's probably worked a total of four hours, maybe less. "Well," he says, "I can think of worse deals."

Delia

DELIA'S LAUGHTER FADES when she turns from Graham to face the bar. Standing just inside the front door of Lilly's is Daniel. He hasn't seen her yet—the bar has gotten rather crowded—but he's scanning the room. He must be out of his mind, Delia thinks. And before she can realign her expression, Graham is following her gaze, and Jon, too. And Daniel is waving and walking toward them, and Graham is thrusting his long arm across the table.

"Danny, old boy!" he shouts.

It all happens so quickly. Daniel starts mumbling some excuse about being in the neighborhood, and Graham is slapping his back and introducing him to Jon, and then, at someone's insistence, Daniel slides into the booth across from her. Who invited him to stay? Was it Graham? Of course it was Graham.

"We've had a head start," Jon says, pouring Daniel a beer in the empty glass they got for Monty. Daniel still hasn't looked her in the eyes.

"So how the hell are you?" Graham asks, as if they're long lost friends.

You must be mistress of any social situation, Delia can hear her late mother saying. *A gathering is only awkward if you allow it to be so.* Well, this is hardly a luncheon on the Vineyard, Mother. Daniel is not a divorcée or a socialist or a Jew.

"I hear you're a writer," Jon says. So Graham *has* told Jon.

And Daniel nods and says something, but it's hard for Delia to hear him through her rage. It is *such bad form* for him to show up like this, she thinks, again channeling her mother's thoughts. What's Monty going to think when he gets here? Did Graham ever think of that?

"He's working on a novel," Graham says. "Big plans, this guy."

Daniel blushes, and his freckled face turns redder than his hair, which gives Delia some measure of relief. He really should leave.

"So, what are you all up to this evening?" Daniel asks.

"Celebrating," Graham replies. "I quit my job this week. Faxed in my old resignation the day we met, in fact."

"Well . . . congratulations," Daniel replies.

"I wonder what's keeping Monty," Delia says, trying to send Graham a meaningful glance.

But to no end. "Monty's a childhood friend of Delia's," Graham says to Daniel. "Short for Richard Rosemont the third. Or fifth. I forget."

"That name sounds familiar," he says.

"Of course you've heard of him," Graham says, his eyes

glowing wickedly, "but please don't make a big deal of it when he gets here. Asking for autographs and such."

"He definitely doesn't go for that kind of thing," Jon adds. "He's a very down-to-earth guy."

So they're going to torture Daniel now. He probably deserves it for showing up like this, though it strikes Delia as a little too easy. But what can she do? The exchange continues, Graham and Jon puffing Monty up into a giant celebrity—teenybopper magazines, movie contracts, Emmy nominations—and Daniel drinks it up. The lies and the beer. He goes through his first pint in five minutes, and tiny little beads of sweat start forming on his forehead. Surely the boys will behave when Monty arrives. Maybe she should send Daniel away. But a scene—that would be worse, and if Monty arrived in the middle—

No point in thinking, because in walks the dear man himself. He came straight from the office, as usual, and the familiarity of his appearance is somehow comforting to Delia. Crisp white shirt, expensive striped tie, and one of those suits with the wide shoulders, which he finally conceded he bought to add size to his small frame. Monty's black hair is parted to the side, and the goatee that punctuates his long, angular face looks as manicured as always.

Delia extends a hand, but Monty doesn't shake or kiss it, so she sweeps the neglected arm into a gesture of introduction. "This is Daniel," she proclaims.

Monty and Daniel face each other for a moment. Then, "I *know* you," Daniel says in wounded triumph. "You work at Sullivan Consulting."

Monty nods gravely and pulls a chair up to the end of the table.

"Well, that's no fun," Graham mutters.

Daniel's whole face drops into a childish pout. Jon rolls his eyes. Graham laughs. And someone has to say something. So Delia does. "It's just a game," she tells Daniel. "Something Jon and I made up eons ago."

"Honey, I think you were still getting carded back then."

"Thanks for that use of the past tense."

"I still get carded," Graham whispers, and Delia turns and sticks out her tongue.

"So you pretend to be famous," Jon explains, "drop names, that sort of thing. Usually we're all famous. We pick characters and go somewhere fabulous and make a huge scene."

"I gather you turned me into the star du jour," Monty says.

Jon shrugs. "Something like that."

"Charming. Did you not get a glass for me?"

And while Monty goes to the bar, Daniel just sits there. What does she think he should say? Finally he comes up with "um," and then, at length, "I get it."

But he doesn't. He's hurt, and it's partly her fault. "Don't be mad," Delia says.

"It's all in good fun," Jon says.

"Sure," Daniel says. And they're all staring at him, which must feel awkward, and his cheeks keep getting redder, his neck too, and finally he stands up and says, "I've got to be going, actually. But, um, it was good to . . . see you all."

"Yeah," Graham says. "Really great to see you again, too."

And Delia feels bad, but it's not as if she's disappointed to see him go. So she waits while he gives the table an uncomfortable nod, and finally Daniel is out the door.

His departure is like a group sigh. The mood lightens almost immediately with recollections of Fame Games going back to her and Graham's conservatory days. Delia happily succumbs to the nostalgia and sinks further into Graham's embrace. He kisses her ear during one of Jon's longer stories, and she rubs her hand up and down Graham's thigh. The warmth of his body through the denim is soothing. His body is always warm. Even on the coldest nights, when her fingertips are like tiny ice cubes, she can snuggle next to him in bed and thaw in his long arms and know that everything is going to be all right.

It's just after midnight when the evening ends, and Delia and Graham walk two blocks in a peaceful silence before Graham says something. "I'm sorry," he says, "for giving that Daniel guy a hard time."

It's a nice sentiment, and Delia squeezes his hand. "No, you're not," she says. "But you're forgiven. And for the record, he's not a bad guy."

"I'm sure he's not," Graham says. "I mean, you obviously have exquisite taste in men."

Delia gives him a playful punch in the arm, and he grabs her fist and kisses it. "No, I'm serious," he says. "I'm sure he's terrific. I promise I'll be much nicer to him next time we see him."

Delia rolls her eyes. "You're a real sport," she says, "but I suspect he's made his last visit to Lilly's."

Daniel

YOU'RE STANDING OUTSIDE of Lilly's when you first hear the scratching again, so you know they're inside. Not that it was such a stretch to assume—it's Saturday night, this is their hangout. But now that you're here, you're a bit less sure of this plan, and you're sweating. Sweating maybe too much. You pace down the sidewalk and stand in front of a Chinese place two doors down. You take a deep breath. You really have no other choice. How else are you going to get back into this book?

The whole day has been agony. And last night, you barely slept. Ended up getting out of bed at six and going for a two-hour run. You were tempted to run all the way to Somerville—hoping, what, that you'd bump into Delia taking out the trash? That would have been more shameful than endearing. You need to have a little more pride. Or less pride. Something like that.

The people in the window seat at the Chinese restaurant

probably wish you would move. You've been leaning against their window, your butt forming a centerpiece for their table. You hadn't noticed. So you give them a smile and an oops-I'm-sorry-have-a-great-evening wave, then slowly walk back toward Lilly's.

You should never have let yourself be pushed off the page so easily. You should have laughed it off last night. Though your fake laugh sounds fake; even you know that. Still, you could have at least *smiled* it off or something.

You practice in a whisper: "Hi, guys, how's it going?" Again, more casually: "Hi, guys. How's it going?" Sounds forced. "What's up, guys?"

What if she's alone?

And then the door opens and almost hits you in the face, and someone holds it open for you, a college girl, maybe, and so you walk into the bar, and there they are, all four of them. The blond guy with the sideburns is talking with his hands. He and Delia are on the bench facing the door, and she's laughing and listening to whatever he's saying. Graham has his back to you, and he must be sitting next to Monty, who's a good head shorter than him and barely visible from the door.

Lilly's is more crowded than it was last night, and you decide to get a drink first. But as you're maneuvering your way toward the bar, you hear behind you, "Is that *Daniel*?"

You turn—they're all staring at you—and walk a few paces to their booth. "Oh, hi, guys," you say. "How's it going?" The word "going" squeaks, like you've hit puberty again, and when you look down, you see that your polo shirt—white, brilliant choice—has a sweat stain right in the middle of your chest.

"It's going all right," the blond guy says.

"What are you up to this evening?" Graham asks, pushing his hair out of his face.

You meet his eyes, then steal a glance at Delia, who appears to be more puzzled by your presence than anything else.

"Just, um, getting a drink," you say. "Thought maybe I'd, ah, come back for an autograph."

This line is met not with laughter but at least with quiet approval. Monty smiles and Delia, too, and you ask if anyone wants something from the bar. Just one taker, the blond guy, whose name is Jon, he reminds you. And there you are, minutes later, with two vodka tonics, pulling up a chair to the end of their table. It all happened so quickly and easily, it's like the author approves of your being here.

"So," Jon says, after a brief silence, "what, ah . . . what did everyone do today?"

"Not much," Monty says. "I went into the office."

Jon turns to you. "Just," you begin, "you know, went to the grocery and stuff."

Jon nods politely. You are a thrill a minute.

"*Someone* told me he was taking me to a zoo," Delia says, resting her arms on the table and giving Graham a conspiratorial grin.

"Down in Dorchester?" Monty asks.

"—but in fact, he took me to Copley Place."

"Which *is* a zoo, if you think about it," Graham says, blowing a cloud of smoke over everyone's heads. "Those women parading through the mall with their long necks and pearls, they might as well be giraffes."

"And the teenage girls in the earring stores, digging in the sale bins, what did we say they were?"

"Groundhogs?"

"No, smaller. They make tunnels in the dirt . . ."

"Ants?" Monty asks.

Jon shrugs. "I'm not a zookeeper, honey."

"Oh, come *on*," Delia says, "what's the name of them?"

And you know what she's talking about. You can picture them. The word is on the tip of your tongue, if you could just find it, if the author would just—

"Gophers?" you say.

"Yes!" she shouts.

"Oh, man," Graham says. "That's right."

"Leave it to the writer," Jon says.

And that word, "gophers," is your most substantial contribution to the evening's festivities, but it seems like enough, because the conversation continues around you without the awkwardness it had yesterday or tonight when you first greeted them. And they're funny, this group, and your laughing seems to spur them on, Graham and Jon especially. And when the evening comes to an end and you start to worry about how you'll meet up with them again, Jon announces Sunday brunch plans without any sign that you're being excluded. So during the good-byes, you duck out early with a quick "See you guys later." That way no one has a chance to clarify one way or the other.

Graham

B<small>UT THAT'S NOTHING</small> compared to the way I met her dad," Graham says, which rouses familiar laughter from all around the brunch table. He knows he's monopolizing the conversation, but he can't stop himself. Besides, everyone seems to be entertained. And so he launches into the story of his first visit to the Jacuzzi at the house where Delia grew up, and she giggles about her father's unexpected arrival during the loudest part of their lovemaking, and Jon laughs as if he's never heard the story before, but of course, he never *has* heard about the timing of her father's appearance because Graham just made up that part. Monty is stroking his goatee with a knowing smile, as if Delia called him the very next morning to tell him how Graham had to hide naked in the linen closet for two hours—although the two hours is a new touch. But it seems to tickle Delia, who is shaking with laughter, and all the while, Daniel listens with what appears to be absolute fascination.

These old stories Graham has been retelling all through the meal are, he'll admit to himself, for Daniel's benefit. Just to clarify that he and Delia have a history, a relationship, a love that can't be set aside after one indiscretion on her part. "I'm Still Here"—that's what Broadway Lady was singing this morning when Graham and Delia were waiting for the train. A rather fitting song for them after the past week. Because he's still here and so is Delia, and that's all Graham is saying. He's not sure who invited Daniel to brunch. He doesn't think it was Delia—was it Monty? Jon?—but hell, in the end, what's the big deal? Graham promised he'd be nice if they ever saw the guy again. Didn't count on seeing him so soon, or often, but Graham has chosen to assume that Daniel is probably just lonely, maybe a little socially inept. Nothing more. So there's no need to play the bad guy or fret over Daniel's presence, but at the same time, why not take the opportunity to make some things clear?

When the sight of half-eaten plates of bacon, remnants of omelets, and unfinished pancakes becomes depressing, Graham suggests the group relocate. They stroll only a few blocks through Harvard Square before settling around one of the bright blue wrought-iron tables at an outdoor café plagued by pigeons and college students. The latter inspires Graham's first get-rich-quick scheme: HMH: Heartwarming Messages Home. The company would help kids ask their parents for money—send loving e-mail messages, make fake receipts for laboratory fees and textbooks, buy little gifts for the kids to mail their parents with notes that say, "This reminded me of you, Mom. Miss you." Daniel seems quite amused by the idea, but Monty thinks there might be some legal issues, and he's probably right.

Now Graham is on his third or fourth idea, and his second or third mimosa. "So then you clamp it into the liner of the window like a cup holder," he explains, "but it's a whole dinner tray with a spot for your drink and a place for your Happy Meal. Why couldn't that work?"

"I'm not saying it couldn't work," Jon says. "Just that someone has probably invented it already."

"Well, I've never seen it," Graham says, tilting his chair back onto its rear legs. "Come on, think. Americans will buy anything made of plastic. We could make millions."

"All you need now is a plastic factory," Monty adds, raising his glass as if for a toast.

With Monty, it's always the manufacturing plants and international distribution centers. "Okay, no factories," Graham says. "Let's go back to services. So, you know how people hate to look for apartments? I could find out what people like and screen apartments for them."

"That's a good idea," Daniel says.

"That's called a rental agent," Monty says. "We have those in this world. But you know, you actually *could* do that, Graham."

"It sounds like a wonderful way to gouge people," Delia says, the bitterness evident beneath her playful tone.

"Hey, if someone's going to profit playing middleman—" Graham begins.

"Now you're sounding a bit too disturbingly like my father," Delia says, "and I assure you, that's not sexy."

No, not the least bit, Graham thinks, crushing out a cigarette and dropping the subject. It's never been clear to him whether Delia's father does anything other than travel to

Asian countries and take commissions on products made in sweatshops, though if Graham is the one to say it, she bites his head off.

"Speaking of my darling father," Delia says to Monty, "not only would he not let me have the pearls for the next Fame Game, but he's decided that I can't touch any of Mom's jewelry. Isn't that cute?" she asks. "My mom died when I was in high school," she adds parenthetically, with a glance toward Daniel. "Of breast cancer."

"I always thought you'd look so nice in that gargantuan ruby ring your grandmother had," Monty says with a chuckle. And then to the group, "You should see some of the things that woman wore."

"Really. Half of it was so gaudy you'd think it had to be fake," Delia says. "Dad has convinced himself that I'd sell all of it if I got my hands on it. And you know, it never occurred to me before he said it, but I think I would. What's the point of holding on to something that had sentimental value fifty years ago? Every clunky brooch could be a few months of freedom."

"That sounds like a fabulous title for a play," Jon announces.

"Indeed," Graham says, thrilled to leave the subject of her father behind. "Delia Benson stars in the hit musical—"

"No, no. It's not a musical," Jon says. "Title's too long. It's a very sad straight play."

"How about 'The Freedom of the Brooch'?" Delia suggests. "That could be a musical."

And this Jon accepts and Daniel, too, but apparently Monty doesn't because he slips away from the table without a word.

"Poor Monty's bitter," Graham tells Daniel. "He was destined to be a gazillionaire. I was destined to make hogs fuck, so sometimes it's nice to escape the trodden path."

"Are you kidding?" Daniel asks.

"No and no," Jon says.

"It's true," Delia says. "Monty and I grew up together. He was a couple years ahead of me in school, and his family's name was on everything. You know Rosemont Park north of Boston? There's even a town called Rosemont where his great grandparents lived. They were one of the richest families in Massachusetts for ages. They can trace their family back to the *Mayflower*."

"But that's about all they can do," Graham says.

"Somehow they lost a lot of the money over the past fifteen or twenty years, bad investments and such, so now . . ."

"He's bitter," Graham says with a grin.

"Who's bitter?" Monty asks, returning to the table.

"You, sir," Graham replies. "For having to work like the common folk."

"Oh, yes, well, it's temporary."

"True. We all die sooner or later," Graham says, pushing his hair behind his left ear.

"My plan," Monty says, without so much as a glance at Graham, "is to make as much money as I possibly can by the time I'm forty-five, then retire to a life of leisure."

"Sounds nice," Daniel says.

"The American Dream," Graham adds. "Riches to Rags to Riches."

Everyone laughs but Monty. "Some people work," he says. "And some of us choose to make as much money as possible with our time so we don't have to work forever."

"I'm with you there," Graham says, offering a solicitous glance around the table. "Plastic lunch trays. How difficult can that be?"

No one replies. Monty is pouting, Delia says something

to Jon, and Daniel's eyes dart back and forth between Delia and Graham. There's something unsettling but familiar about the look in Daniel's eyes now that he's not laughing or smiling or agreeing with everything. A hunger. The guy is studying them. It's like he's making mental notes. Graham can almost feel his energy being sucked away.

"We should pay," Graham says before he realizes the words are coming out. And after they take care of the bill and exchange good-byes, Graham hurries Delia down to the train before anyone can suggest another plan that includes Daniel.

Daniel

THIS DOESN'T SEEM like the kind of book you'd want to read. There's so much talk. You prefer books like the new Richard Corrone novel that you've set across the table from you as an incentive. If you can just get through the damned presentation you promised to have ready for Monday, you can dive back into it. Now Corrone can write a novel. The last one ended with a renegade CIA agent imprisoned in a secret Communist stronghold in Switzerland, of all places. The sequel has gotten great press. Of course, the agent makes a dramatic escape in the first chapter, which you quickly skimmed before setting the book aside. At least you don't have to feel too bad about skipping today's run after an afternoon of drinking. There probably won't be any elaborate chase scenes in this book.

You're at the coffee shop in Cambridge Books, trying not to think about Delia or Graham or brunch this morning or Richard

Corrone. There's a lot in your head right now. Which is why it's always useful to have a notebook. You look down at the rather bad ideas you've come up with for how an Italian bank can enter the U.S. market. Bank Rome, they want to call it. This is what you need to think about. You were not destined to be a gazillionaire, so you need to do some work.

Rome. . . . You're going to have to go with the personality, the charm of Italy. Columns and wine and olive groves. Maybe some sensual angle. Red. And white for the columns. Green for the hillside . . . like the flag. Oh, you are a genius. Why is an Italian bank trying to move into the U.S. anyway? Italy is not exactly regarded as a financial center of the world.

You really can't concentrate. The man at the table beside you keeps dropping books on the floor, and you want someone to tell him that this isn't a library. He's just come back with another stack of about twelve. And though you didn't notice before, he appears to be a writer, or so his selections suggest: *The Complete Guide to Character Traits*, *20 Plots That Never Fail*, *Mastering Fiction*, *Novel-Writing from A to Z*. The man is hunched over one of the books, and you go for a refill of coffee so you can steal a glance at his laptop. It's hard to see, but you catch the phrase "Thorgon speaks" near the top of the screen.

For some reason, the words make you uneasy, and when you get back to your table, you find yourself thinking about brunch this morning and drinks last night and Delia's hurried departure today and Graham kissing her in the bedroom doorway the other morning. And all of it makes you feel like an ass. Maybe you're just humiliating yourself. Maybe you're not wanted in this book. Maybe you've served your purpose—as some prop in a fight between Graham and Delia—and now you're overstaying your welcome. But then you don't want to let another chance pass you by. How many times in your life can you expect to hear—

You hear it now. The scratching is in the bookstore. It's pretty loud, actually. You scan the tables nearby, but no, the sound isn't coming from another table. It's focused on you.

Incredible. In five days, you've gone from a nobody in the background of Lilly's to someone the author wants to follow. It's exciting to have achieved this status so quickly. But also kind of intimidating. You are at a bookstore, after all. What are you supposed to do to keep the author's attention? Read? No one wants to read about someone reading. People want to read about a guy doing something. All you're doing now is staring at your coffee mug, a plain white coffee mug.

Again, you survey the tables around you. There's the aspiring novelist, some college kids studying, an old couple, two women across the room having an argument. You could eavesdrop. It's tempting. If you were alone, you might. You can just make out what they're saying. You've always had a pretty keen sense of hearing. Could hear your parents' hushed conversations through their bedroom door: about money and winnings and loans and your Cs in algebra. Hushed conversations, and other sounds a kid probably shouldn't hear. You had a girlfriend a few years back who found that little skill of yours amusing— until one night you overheard her talking on the phone in the other room, and that pretty much ended things. You honestly thought she was ordering pizza, just wondered what toppings she was getting. Turned out she met a guy at a conference; they actually got married later. It was a shame. She was the only woman you ever dated who left an extra bottle of contact lens solution at your place.

The scratching is still with you, quieter but there. The author is waiting for something to happen.

"But what?" you whisper.

A couple of teenage girls look at you and mumble something

to each other. Okay, stop talking to yourself. Think. Is Delia going to show up? Or someone else? Or is this moment all about you? It's impossible to figure this out. You really could use some help. You write that down in your notebook: "I really could use some help." Somehow, writing the words is a relief. Nothing happens, though. But what do you expect? Do you think the old woman two tables over is going to take your hand and walk you through the process? *On Tuesday, Mr. Fischer, you'll need to go down to a diner on Mass. Ave. . . .* This is ridiculous. You glance over at the writer hiding behind his tower of books. And you see that one of the manuals is written by Richard Corrone.

The discovery feels significant.

You find yourself walking through the bookstore as if driven—and you are driven, aren't you? Of course you are. The scratching of the pencil grows louder as you walk, and in a minute or so, you're standing in the reference section which has four shelves of books on writing and marketing. Almost immediately you spot the one by Corrone: *15 Steps to Writing a Bestseller.* You pick up the book, but you don't open it at first. It might not be the right book. The author guided you here, certainly, but then there are dozens of other manuals. How will you know which one to use? And yet they're all creations of the author if they're in this world, and here you are holding this one. If this is the one you picked up, it must be the right book.

You look at the table of contents: fifteen chapter titles like Chinese fortune cookies for the writer, things like "Never Start at the Beginning" and "Let the Truth Reveal Itself." The words are at once comforting and terrifying. Is this the author's way of talking to you? You flip through the book and stop at random in the middle of a chapter. "Plant the Seeds, Then Water the Garden," the chapter is called. "You have to allow the characters time to take shape," Corrone says. "Give the seeds room to grow." What does that even mean?

You carry the manual back to the coffee area, where the man with the pile of books is pounding away at the Thorgon story. You need to study this book. And you need to get the Bank Rome presentation ready for Monday. But with the author watching? You wonder if Thorgon ever wants to reach through the computer screen and ask this guy for a little privacy. You don't want the author to abandon you. Definitely not that. "Just a break," you whisper into your hand.

Delia

T HE LIVER SPOT on Mr. Demarco's left cheekbone is shaped like Great Britain.

"Uh-huh," Delia says with a big smile.

And the one on his chin looks kind of like a turkey. Or a chicken. It's hard to say.

"*Really?*"

He's telling her about his career in the cutlery business. It doesn't sound so bad, Delia muses. Going door to door in an age when people actually opened the door, invited you in, offered you a glass of tea, and weighed the merits of your cutlery against those of the leading brand. That's how he says he met his wife. It's a sweet story, but sometimes Mr. Demarco gets confused and thinks he's talking about the woman who gives out cans of Ensure at snack time.

"You *did*?" she asks, urging him on. He's not talking to her so much as to her breasts. Mr. Demarco likes to look at Delia's breasts. In all fairness, he likes to look at her face, too, but she is perched on a stool that puts her breasts closer to his eye level. He sits in his wheelchair in the common room of the Methodist Home. They're finishing up lunch. Running a bit late, in fact, and Delia only has forty minutes left before she'll be expected back at the office. She glances around the room to catch the eye of a staff member, but to no avail. They're all wiping food from the mouths of the residents or feeding those who need more assistance.

"I can't *believe* it!" Delia says at a pause in Mr. Demarco's narrative.

Why does she do this to herself, play the part of a good, caring person? She won't dare mention these visits to Graham, let alone Monty, who'd be appalled. But does it really make a difference if she listens or not?

"I'll bet she is beautiful," Delia tells him, not sure whether they're discussing the wife or Ensure lady at the moment.

He says Delia is beautiful, too, and this makes her smile. She *is* helping him, after all. And so what if she gets something out of the experience, too. It's good of her to come here, even if she can't explain it to anyone, even if part of her is embarrassed, even if—

"Delia," a nurse says, "we're ready for you."

She excuses herself from Mr. Demarco's table, points to the small platform with the microphone by way of explanation, decides the liver spot definitely looks more like a chicken, then heads to the front of the room. It's been five weeks since she last held a microphone in her hands. The last time she sang in public, it was here. The time before that, here. Before that . . . may have been at the Crib on karaoke night, but it was still exhilarating. Nice to keep the vocal cords working until things turn around.

Dishes clink, old people cough and chatter.

"Hello again, everyone."

The chatter subsides for a moment.

"My name is Delia Benson. Many of you may remember me. I'm here today to sing a couple of songs for you while you finish up lunch."

Someone at the table in front of her cries out for more corn. A nurse is paged over the loudspeaker.

"I'd like to start with a song I used to love to sing in school," she says, "but unfortunately, my teachers thought it was dated—"

A plate crashes to the floor. One nurse goes to clean it up. Another carries a bowl of creamed corn past Delia and sets it down in front of Mrs. Weinberg.

"—dated and not very challenging," Delia continues. She bites her lip and looks at the floor, then spots a hazy puddle and forces her eyes up again. The crowd of tables reappears in a slight blur, but when she blinks, the room returns to focus. "Anyway, um, I think if you listen carefully to the words, this song . . . this song tells a very powerful story well worth a musician's efforts."

Delia nods to the nursing aide at the piano beside the platform, and the music begins like a player piano in a 1940s saloon. When Delia performed this song at a high school talent contest, she wore a tattered violet dress, heavy makeup, and a bright blond wig. Today, she's wearing a gray skirt and black cotton blazer. She wishes she'd at least brought a flower for her hair, but then as the piano vamps to her entrance, it doesn't matter. This is the good feeling. The lump in her throat recedes.

Do you know Rose?
She sings on Sunday nights.
We stop the jukebox
To hear her song.

And Delia is on the stage at her high school, where the audience roars with applause, where her mother rushes backstage to kiss her again and again and Monty waits outside with a dozen roses.

There was a time she led a
Small-time band. The
Whole town knew her
Then.

And now Delia is auditioning for the New England Conservatory. A Billie Holiday song. They love her. The head of the department insists on being her vocal coach. And on the weekends, she performs at weddings and at clubs. Then Graham arrives, the mysterious pianist who shed his Texan drawl. He becomes her accompanist, and they stay up late with Jon and Monty, and they laugh and laugh. And now it's her junior recital, and the auditorium is packed, and the people in the front row are crying. Crying for Rose.

Rose made a record once
But no one played it.
No one paid a dime.

The pianist's fingers slip, then recover, bringing Delia back to the Methodist Home, where nobody is listening. Not even Mrs. Weinberg, who once said Delia looks like Natalie Wood, although she doesn't, not really.

Do you know Rose?

And the years pass without notice until Delia is eighty and gumming creamed corn. And a playwright visits her in the Methodist Home and decides to write the story of a girl who sells lupus and never does anything she wants to do past the age of twenty-one. But he won't even let Delia play the part.

Then came the time when the
Whole band crumbled,
World came tumbling
Down.

She can feel a tear running down her cheek, but she's getting through the song. Her voice cracks once, but only once. Twice now. Think of something else. Graham's watery blue eyes, picking up Myra as a kitten from that house in Woburn, the surprise party two months before her twentieth birthday, that weekend at the beach when their car broke down.

Do you know Rose?

The vocal coach telling her she needs more classical training, that her vibrato is too pronounced, that she should learn to like opera, that she's ruining her voice singing in smoky bars, that she's not training hard enough. Her father saying she needs to support herself, then her damned cyst, his ill-ness—and it's almost a relief not to have to go to New York to see what will happen, but at the same time, it's not. And she and Graham are so poor. And then Graham dropping that bomb on her, saying he just wants to try this out—and he's impossible to talk to, so finally she says it's okay, think-ing he'll never go through with it. But then waiting at home for him and wondering every time he's out late. And then finally that night with Daniel . . .

Do you know Rose?
She sits home every night,
Except on Sundays
We hear her song.

Some people clap. Many cough. Mrs. Weinberg beams up at Delia, but Delia has seen her clap with the same en-thusiasm for a puppet show. Mr. Demarco has been wheeled out. And as much as Delia wants to run out the door and straight home, she does not. Nor does she offer to sing a second song; she seldom does. She just slips into the cafeteria bathroom, which reeks of urine and bleach, and fixes her eye shadow, adds powder to her cheeks, and applies another layer of bright red lipstick. Then she closes her eyes, takes several deep breaths, and she pushes out the overlapping images that are crowding her mind.

"Did I get any messages?" she says to her reflection. No, that doesn't sound natural at all. She forces a smile. "Any calls while I was out?" That's better. She can do it. She can return to her office, and she can call twenty-eight more people today to ask them to consider increasing their annual support to the two-hundred-dollar level.

Daniel

Y OU'RE BACK AT Lilly's because Corrone says that if you put characters together in a room, something is bound to happen. But unfortunately, no one is here with you. Well, no one you want to see. The place is actually packed. It's Friday night, and you couldn't get a booth, so you're sitting on a stool at the bar beside a man who spent twenty minutes telling you about an extramarital affair before concluding, "It's not really cheating. Not if you think about it."

To ward off further conversation, you have assumed a posture of deep concentration, but more than an hour has passed, and you're starting to feel particularly conspicuous sitting here nursing a now-tepid pint of beer with your notebook opened before you. You don't feel inspired to work. The Rome team wants something to do with history, but the only thing you've come up with tonight is "Rome: Managing Money Since Before Christ." So you've abandoned Rome, and to appear busy, you keep scrib-bling down the lyrics of the songs that come on. And what's in-teresting, but also a little disconcerting, is that there seem to be specific messages of failure in each song you transcribe: "It's all over now." "I'll be gone." "Don't come back to me."

Coming here seemed like a better idea earlier this evening. You drink the last few ounces of your beer during a break be-tween songs, and you're considering going home, but that's when you hear it. The scratching. It's right on top of you.

"Taking care of business?" asks the man beside you.

You shouldn't have looked up because you do not want to talk to this man. You have a lot on your mind, and you are not in the market for new friends or new characters to introduce to the author or—

Actually, you could make some use of this man. "Do you hear something?" you say.

"Hear what, man? Them?" he asks, nodding at the table be-hind you.

"No, that sound," you say. "Like a scratch, like the sound of a pencil writing."

The man concentrates with the intensely furrowed brows that only three consecutive whiskeys can provide. Then he shakes his head. "Sorry, man. You're the sole receiver. Is it like a ringing in your ear? 'Cause I hate that."

Now the stereo starts up again, some acoustic band you don't recognize.

"You think it's radio waves?" the man asks. "Or microwaves? There's so many fucking waves these days."

"That's true," you say.

"I wonder if short waves and long waves sound different. Maybe everyone picks up different waves, and the ones you hear sound different from the ones I hear. You think?"

"Could be."

You've always wanted to ask someone. You can't very well ask Delia. And you couldn't ask your parents that time you went out to dinner with them and overheard a couple being written a few tables away. This was about eight years ago, on your twenty-third birthday, in fact. Your parents were going on and on about some new casino going up in Las Vegas, and you weren't trying to tune them out. But the restaurant was quiet, and this couple was having such a tense conversation, and then the scratching started right above them. Just as things were getting serious, too. The guy was begging for a second chance, and the woman was saying she couldn't trust him anymore. It sounded like a pivotal moment in their book. You listened— nodding occasionally during your parents' tag-team narrative— and it felt odd knowing that you were just part of the scenery, just filling a table while this couple's story was being written.

It was only after you got home that it occurred to you that you didn't *have* to stay in the background the whole time the author's pencil was scratching. You could have walked up to their table and offered some advice. Not that people really do that kind of thing, but you could have. Or you could have followed one of them into the lobby and said something outside the bathrooms. You could have sent a message through the waiter, or passed by the table and tripped over the woman's handbag. If you'd made a real effort, you could have been important to them. And their book.

You actually had been important in a book once before— without even trying. Of course, that was the first time you ever heard the scratching sound, so you didn't fully understand what was happening. It was a weeknight during your senior year in college. You'd left a party at a friend's apartment on Newbury Street and were walking back to your dorm. It was probably three in the morning, so the train had stopped running hours ago, and there weren't any cabs in sight. The walk never took more than thirty minutes, so you didn't mind. The street was empty, and you felt like the only person in the city.

But then, in a blur of storefronts, your body was yanked into a shadowy alcove, your face slammed against a glass door, and your spine jabbed with the hard nose of a revolver. There were two of them, both short, slim, and wearing ski masks. They were girls. About fifteen or sixteen. The one with the gun felt like she was trying to burrow a hole in your back. The other one fished into your pockets and pulled out your wallet.

You could feel a thin stream of blood drip slowly from your nose to your lips, and you wondered if it would hurt, being shot. Probably depended on where the bullet hit. You tried to remember which organs were where, remember as if you once knew, but of course, you didn't. Not that they were going to shoot you, you told yourself. That couldn't happen.

"He's got twelve dollars."

"I'm gonna blow his brains out."

You opened your eyes. You were facing a leather goods store, a sale rack of purses just inside the door.

"You got anything else? A watch?"

You extended your arm and let her remove the watch from your wrist.

"Piece of shit. That's not worth anything. You know he's got the good stuff at home. I want to shoot him. Wasting my time."

"You can't kill him."

"Why not?"

And this began a rather extended discussion about the implications of killing you. While you stood there, staring at the purses, noticing that some of them actually cost more than a thousand dollars—on sale—the wallet girl was explaining to the gun girl that no one in the world cared if they robbed you. But if they killed you, then everyone would start to care. "And plus," she said, "it's a slippy slope."

"What the fuck you mean?"

"You kill one guy 'cause you're pissed off, you gonna kill another."

These girls were having a moment. It felt more choreographed than real. You even thought that at the time. You started out as some random person they were robbing, someone they didn't think of as having a life or an existence independent of that moment, and then suddenly you became a symbol, a choice, a turning point. So when the gun girl pressed the revolver harder into your spine and you heard yourself whisper, "No," you were speaking for her best interests as well as your own.

You waited, listening to the breathing of the girls, the cars a few streets away, and a sound in the air that you couldn't place. Then, "Fuck it," the girl said, and you felt her pull the gun away. Suddenly your knees were buckling and the girls were running, the slap of their footsteps fading into the distance along with that other sound. And yes, it sounded like a pencil. It even crossed your mind that this was the kind of event that might be written. But you didn't think anything more of it until a few months later when you were going for a run in Boston Commons and heard the scratching around a family picnic. You circled back a few times to be sure, stopped to stretch, got a bottle of water, and sat down nearby. There was a good-bye in the works—a lot of hugging and awkward laughing, a few tears, something significant—and above it all hovered this familiar noise. When everyone packed up to leave, you stood up, too, and followed the sound as it followed the family down the block and into a taxicab. You understood the moment their cab pulled away.

Two years later, you heard the scratching again when that couple was being written at the restaurant. Then there was the teenage kid about a year and a half after that, but he took off on a bike almost as soon as you spotted him. It wasn't until you were twenty-eight that you noticed a man being written in a department store. You followed him for half an hour, trying to think of what to do, hoping someone might try to abduct him or something so you might have an obvious point of entry. But then he walked out into the shopping mall, and it was loud and you couldn't hear the scratching clearly, and eventually you lost him. That was three years ago. Then you found Delia, and here you are on the page.

But why are you on the page *now?* At this minute. At Lilly's. Corrone says everything must happen for a reason. Maybe you were supposed to ask your drinking buddy here about the sound and then remember the mugging and all that so it could get written. What Corrone calls "backstory." That's kind of clever. Or maybe—

"Daniel?"

It's Delia. She's right beside you, picking up a pitcher of beer. Behind her, the man who says he isn't actually cheating on his wife gives you a thumbs up.

"What are you up to?" she asks. "Are you working?"

You hurriedly close the notebook, and Delia's eyes follow the gesture. You wonder if she's going to make fun of you for working on Friday night—but no, you're a writer. It's different. It's pretentious and profound to be sitting at a bar writing. So you nod, say yes.

"Well, look who's here!" It's Graham, and he follows the greeting with a hard slap on your shoulder.

"If you want to take a break," Delia adds, "you're welcome to join us."

The booth they've claimed is just two away from the one where you and Delia first met. You slide in across from them, and Graham pours the beer, and as he's handing you a pint, he asks you to tell him about your book. You say there's not much to tell yet, you're just starting. "But what's it *about?*" he presses. And you don't really have an answer for him, so you use a phrase from Corrone and say that you're still "settling into the characters."

"I do make at least a cameo, don't I?" Delia asks with a dramatic blink of her eyes. You blanch, but almost instantly she waves the question away. "Don't answer that," she says. "I'm sure Monty's darling Natalie will put me in one of her books as a raving bitch who kills her children and eats them over couscous."

Graham claps his hands and chuckles, and you say, "So what about you guys? Do you perform much?"

"Nah," Graham says, "not these days."

"We did a lot in school," Delia adds, "and right after."

"You both went to the New England Conservatory, right?"

"For a while," she says.

"But we threw our education away," Graham adds. "Isn't that what they said?"

Delia rolls her eyes. "I was insufficiently loved."

"They were trying to turn her into something she wasn't, and I hated all the recitals and the bullshit, so we left after two years to work on our own stuff—well, three years for Delia, two for me." Graham pulls out a pack of rolling papers and an envelope of tobacco. "We started to put together a jazz act," he continues, "and I was writing some stuff. We did a bunch of weddings and local gigs, and we were going to move to New York, but—what happened?"

"Well, you wanted some time to write music, and then there was the gigantic cyst on my ovary."

"Right. And then your father's fictitious heart attack."

"It wasn't a fictitious heart attack."

"Well, it wasn't a heart attack."

"Dad thought he had a heart attack," Delia explains, "and he was scared for a while, so I didn't want to move right then."

"It was gas," Graham tells you.

"It wasn't gas! It was like a murmur or something. I can't remember."

"He just didn't want you to go. It was psychosomatic."

"Probably," Delia says. "Oh, did I tell you about my visit with him on Wednesday?"

"No," Graham says.

"He was in Boston for the gun show—my father collects guns," she tells you, topping off your glass.

"Is he a hunter?" you ask.

"No," Graham replies. "He's crazy."

"He did hunt when I was growing up," Delia says, "but now he pretty much just likes guns. My mother had a china cabinet where she kept her wedding china, and Dad took all that out a couple of years after she died and filled it with antique guns. He keeps a pistol in his night table and one in a kitchen cabinet, too, right behind the bread box. Visiting him is like some morbid scavenger hunt. But anyway," she says, turning back to Graham, "do you know what he told me? He told me that he'd seen a program on television about Ecstasy, and he wanted me to know that it causes permanent brain damage."

Graham's laughter seems out of proportion to the joke, if that's what it is.

"Why did he tell you that?" you ask.

"To be helpful. My father has always had a very positive image of me."

The evening progresses pretty smoothly, except for that

one moment when you ask Graham about his parents. "I hate them" is all he says, but he says it with a smile, so you can't tell if he's serious. Still, there's a long pause after that, and it makes you uncomfortable with the author there, so you decide to tell them about the time your father tried to get you to join his bowling league. Because people usually like that story. But maybe you tell it wrong this time because it doesn't go over very well. But then when you tell them about the poker game where your parents lost the family station wagon to your school bus driver, Graham goes into a fit of hysterics that's contagious, so by the end, you're all three laughing wildly. You don't think the story was *that* funny, but you're glad they like it.

All in all, they seem much more relaxed around you tonight. Like seeing you isn't an ordeal but more a matter of course. Like they want you to be in their group. Delia even asks you for your phone number and invites you to go see a show next weekend. Between the invitation and the attention you've been getting from the author, it feels like you really have secured a role in Delia's book, and that's a good feeling to drive home with. But then as you pull onto your street, Graham's question returns to you and your sense of security fades. Because how can you be sure of your role if you don't know what the book is about?

Monty

SITTING BEFORE A half dozen tiny plates of marinated olives, sautéed asparagus, bell pepper salad, and chicken curry, surrounded by the tall lavender walls and violet drapery of the tapas bar, everyone at the table appears to Monty as if they've dressed for different occasions. He chose the opening night of *Fragile* to wear his new navy Brooks Brothers suit, which roused immediate and satisfying admiration from Natalie. The shoulders are slightly squared and help keep him from looking so skinny, and the pinstripes complement Natalie's pale blue silk evening dress. She's wearing especially high heels tonight, which Monty finds a bit thoughtless since they make her so much taller than him, but otherwise she looks lovely. Her grandmother's pearls sit handsomely on her long neck, and sparkling through her chestnut hair are the small sapphire earrings he gave her last

Christmas. Jon complimented Natalie on the earrings during the intermission, and Monty appreciated that. It's not
always easy to make her feel welcome with this group.

At the theater, Monty must have been too distracted by
Natalie's presence and the excitement of the crowd and Jon's
last-minute arrival to notice, but the disparity of everyone's
attire is quite evident in the light of the tapas bar. Graham
wears a red plaid shirt with a black sport coat, the same
shapeless sport coat Monty has seen him wear to every play,
recital, and performance since the boy appeared at the conservatory at the age of sixteen. Beside him sits Delia in a red
satin thrift-store number with a black scarf and clutch purse.
She might as well have stepped onto the stage at the theater.
But for all Delia's bohemian pretense, Monty will have to
point out to Natalie that the boots she's wearing probably
cost her father more than Monty's new suit. It is a nice suit,
though the lint it attracts is a bit tiresome.

Jon's look is fairly tame tonight. He can actually pull off
that canary yellow polo shirt with his dark tan and the blond-
ish hair, but those dangerously-close-to-white pants should
not be brought out until after Memorial Day. And yet, one
can't very well wear corduroy in June. No, the pants should
never have been made. But better that he's opted for corduroys rather than the leather pants he wore last time Natalie
visited. She had a lot to say about those. She can be a little
unforgiving when it comes to Monty's friends.

Of course, these are all Delia's acquisitions. She's always
collected interesting types. Even when they were in high
school, she picked up the Waverly twins and that boy who
played the tuba and peddled dope. And what ever happened
to the painter, the fellow with the mustache whose sordid
sense of humor Monty liked to pretend he found offensive?

The guy was with them all last summer, then disappeared without anyone's commenting.

This latest acquisition is a little perplexing. Daniel is dressed inoffensively in beige slacks and a blue blazer, white shirt, no tie. Coppery red hair, freckles everywhere. Monty assumed he was a temporary diversion a couple of weekends ago, but apparently Delia and Graham had drinks with him last weekend, too. For what reason, Monty cannot guess. Daniel doesn't speak much, and when he does, he seldom says anything clever. Natalie's writer friends in New York never stop telling stories, but Daniel mostly just listens and laughs at the right moments . . . not a bad quality in itself. Perhaps Delia keeps him around to give Graham a fresh audience. Lord knows, Monty is tired of hearing him hold court. How she's put up with him for six years is a mystery. Slumming is cute in college, but it becomes less endearing with time.

Natalie can't stand Graham, though she's not such a fan of Delia, either. But then Delia is seldom very kind to women. Ever since Natalie offered the slightest criticism of tonight's play, Delia has been defending every line, movement, and note of incidental music in the show, and Jon, coming to her aid, has pronounced it the next *Who's Afraid of Virginia Woolf?*

"I thought you said that thing at the Shubert was the next *Who's Afraid of Virginia Woolf?*" Monty says.

"Well, this is the next one after that," Jon replies.

"I'm just saying his last play was clearly superior," Natalie explains. "Don't you agree, Mont?"

"*Mont?*" Delia says.

"It was very good," he replies, avoiding Delia's eyes. He can't recall the show, but he and Natalie often go to the theater when he visits her in New York. If he hated the show, Monty would definitely remember it.

"It got tremendous reviews," Natalie continues.

"Well, then it must have been brilliant," Delia says. "Jon, did you see it?"

Jon shrugs. "It was all right, but it was playing at the same time as *Madison,* which you know I *fell in love* with—I wanted that play to bear my children—so everything else I saw that trip kind of paled in comparison."

"I liked *Madison,*" Monty agrees. "I thought it was coming to Boston."

"No," Jon replies. "It was trashed in the papers right after I saw it. Closed the next week."

"God, I hate reviewers," Delia announces at a volume sufficient to inform the people at the next table. "Why do people need to be told what they should like?"

"Because people are cows," Graham replies.

It's a script Monty has heard before and one that grows tiresome with repetition.

"Did you say you're an actor?" Daniel asks Jon. God bless him for changing the subject.

"Oh, no. I used to act, but no, I don't anymore."

"We met doing a show together," Delia tells Daniel, her words starting to slur. Monty hasn't said anything about it yet, but he does think she's been drinking a little too much these days.

"Why did you stop?" Daniel says to Jon.

It takes a minute before Jon replies. He's surveying the bar, cruising the room, Monty knows. Does it every time Natalie is here. "Oh, who can remember?" Jon says to Daniel with a wink. "I think it interfered with my social life." A moment later, Jon is across the room talking to a young man with glasses and a strange flip to his hair. They'll be having sex within the hour, Monty is certain. It's a good thing Natalie isn't as observant as she could be. Maybe that's what Daniel does, studies people and looks for material. Natalie's poetry all seems to be about herself, but some writers eavesdrop, take things from the world around them.

The conversation has moved on without Monty. "It's a known fact," Natalie is saying. "He toured Italy, joined the Boston Philharmonic, and then he went off on his own."

Oh dear, she's talking about the Powell book. Monty's circle generally avoids all reference to office activity, but Natalie doesn't like to abide by this unspoken rule. In fairness, the publishing world in which she lives does tend to have more interesting material than Monty's or Delia's or Jon's. And what would Graham know about a job?

"People lie on their resumes," Graham is saying. "All the time. That's how half the people in this country get jobs. That's the American way."

"Well, of course they lie," Monty offers, "but in this case it's true. The editors verify everything before they'll publish a book. Isn't that right, Natalie?"

"Not everything, but I'm sure they'd verify the fact that he played in the Philharmonic before they'd let him write a book about it."

"That's what I should do," Graham proclaims. "Write an exposé about the Boston Philharmonic or something. Just totally make shit up. Will you publish that, too?"

Daniel laughs on cue. Delia laughs, too, but she's clearly pretending.

"Daniel's a writer," Monty volunteers, and this sentence seems to deflate Graham.

"Really?" Natalie says.

"He's writing a *novel*," Delia announces with glassy eyes.

"That's wonderful," Natalie says. "Have I read any of your books?"

"Oh, no," Daniel says, shaking his head.

"Any stories published?"

Daniel's face is turning almost as red as Graham's shirt, which is saying a great deal. "Nowhere special," he says at last.

"But you have?" Natalie says. "Where?"

All eyes have turned to Daniel, who doesn't appear to relish the attention. It takes him some time to get the words out. "Just some small magazines," he finally says. "*The Violet Stream* and, um, *Wisconsin Review*."

"The *Wisconsin Review*," Natalie repeats. "That's nothing to sneeze at."

"Oh," he says, twisting the stem of his glass. "But it was a while ago. I'm just getting back into things."

"Well, good for you," she says. "When you finish your book, I'd love to see it."

"Natalie's an associate editor for Random House," Monty tells Daniel. "Used to work for the *Harvard Review*."

Daniel's gaze falls to the table. "That's great," he says.

"I know a lot of people," Natalie tells him. "I'd love to help if I can."

"Marvelous," Delia mumbles.

Monty knows it's coming before he feels Natalie start tapping his knee under the table. That's her exit sign. So Monty takes care of the check and says his good-byes, and he's a little surprised when neither Graham nor Delia says anything about getting together for Sunday brunch. It could be on account of Natalie's presence, but it might also be because of Daniel. Delia can be fickle. It's just as well, because Monty would rather keep Natalie to himself for the rest of her visit. As it is, she's going to spend the next two hours asking him what he sees in these people.

"Your writer friend seemed nice," she says to Monty as they walk to the car. "I'll have to look up his stories when I get back."

Daniel

THE SCRATCHING IS in your apartment now. It woke you up. And yet it's five in the morning. You only got back from the tapas bar three hours ago, and your body does not want to move from the bed. It's nice to know the author thinks you're worth this kind of attention, but so early? Is something exciting supposed to happen at this hour? Maybe this is a warning. Someone's going to call. But then the phone could wake you up. Or maybe someone's about to stop by, but no, then the doorbell could just ring. Unless—

Unless someone's breaking in. Now the adrenaline starts pumping. You reach into your night table and grab the flashlight—not the oh-no-the-power's-out flashlight but the one-crash-on-your-skull-and-your-brain's-oozing-out-your-ears billy club of a flashlight. You move silently to the bedroom door and flip on the light in the living room. No one creeping about or hiding behind the beige sofa or armchair. The scratching follows you as you slink across the living room and poke your head into the kitchen. It's empty, too. You live on the second floor of a multifamily house, and you don't hear any movement on the floor above you or below. Nothing from the apartment next door. You peer out the living room window but see nothing but the quiet street. So really you're just walking around in the dark in your boxers holding a flashlight like a baseball bat. And all this is being written.

And meanwhile, the apartment is a wreck. You're glad for the author's return, but you were hardly prepared for company. You pull the sweat-soaked gym clothes off the shower rod and cram them into a laundry bag, run a washcloth over the counter to pick up stray hairs from your razor. In the mirror, you see your hair is standing up in all directions, and your freckled chest has a large imprint of the sheets across it. So you grab a T-shirt and a pair of sweatpants off the floor, your Red Sox cap from the top of your dresser. You pick up the rest of the clothes, make your bed. You're tempted to deal with the pile of dishes in the kitchen, but you resist the urge because now this is getting ridiculous. You finally have the author recording your every move, and here you are cleaning the apartment.

You feed water and grounds to the coffeemaker, toss a frozen bagel into the microwave, then sit down at the table. The scratching is still with you, faint but steady. You need to figure this out. If the author wants to describe your apartment, you don't have to be here for that. Don't have to be awake. Clearly you're supposed to *do* something. But what? "I can't read your mind," you say to the air around you. "Could you give a sign or something?"

The coffeemaker burbles. The microwave bings. What did you expect? You take a bite of the bagel, which tastes vaguely of glue and sponge. Takes some resolve to chew. You get a plate, sit down again. You have to get a handle on your role. Man-Who-Drinks-With-Others is not going to cut it. You need to take a more active part.

But then, how active is *anyone* in this book? They sound like such talented people, but no one's performing or auditioning or really doing anything. Instead, they sit around talking about inventing plastic travel accessories. That's all anyone does, sits around and talks. What kind of book is this? Not one that gets made into a movie, that's for sure. A break-in actually might have been cool. Kind of irrelevant, but exciting nonetheless.

You pour yourself a cup of coffee, and when you sit down again, your eyes drift over a pile of magazines on the floor. The scratching gets louder. Slowly, you drop to your knees and sift though the pile, and when your hand falls on last month's issue of *Boston* magazine, the pencil makes two loud strokes. It's a special music issue. The headline reads, "Michael Powell's Rise from Obscurity to Stardom." Lower down, you see the caption "Music Reviews: The Best CDs You've Never Heard." The scratching has intensified all around you, and you burst out laughing.

"You don't mince words, do you?" you say, glancing up at the ceiling.

Michael Powell is the blues musician Graham and Natalie were discussing last night, so you take the magazine to the sofa to read the review of Powell's memoir. Powell played the saxophone in tiny blues bands, filled in for a friend playing clarinet on a concert tour of Italy and Switzerland, then got a call from the Boston Philharmonic. He hated the conductor there and wanted to play the sax again, so on his nights off, Powell returned to the clubs and invited every agent, promoter, reviewer, and record executive he could think of to see him play.

For the most part, none came, but eventually he got a couple of good reviews which led an intern at a record company to stop by one of his gigs. One year later, he had a CD on the top of the charts. Nice story. Powell had the requisite ambition.

Magazine in hand, you sit down at the computer in your living room and begin typing a review for a fictitious concert by Graham. You date the article two years back and set the concert in one of the smaller clubs listed in the "What's Happening" section of the magazine. At first, it's difficult to write, but then you begin lifting phrases like "vibrant melodics" and "thunderous crescendos" from the music review section, and the review practically writes itself. See, you are a fiction writer after all. It's really a lot like marketing anything else—a bank, a software company, a brand of shoes. You just have to get the lingo right.

You keep the next two reviews short so you can attribute them to staff writers at *Boston* magazine and the *Boston Globe*. In the final review, you use every impressive word that didn't fit into any of the previous articles—including 8-across, "contrapuntal," and 22-down, "sonority," from *Boston* magazine's crossword puzzle—and you credit both this and the first review to a couple of local music rags you find on the Internet. Altogether, the articles take you just a few hours to write. The letter from Graham's agent takes another hour or so, and there are some holes to fill in, but by the time you start looking online for the mailing and e-mail addresses of the smaller concert halls and music producers outside of Boston, you feel pretty pleased with yourself.

This is going to be a stranger-comes-to-town-and-shows-them-the-way book. Plot Number 12 or 13 on Corrone's list. And you're the stranger—that's a good part. So first you'll get Graham to start auditioning for things. He has more free time than anyone—he's unemployed, he needs the work. Then after he starts getting a few breaks, Delia will be so encouraged, Jon too, that they'll start performing again. Graham might be able to help them get work, or you can pose as their talent agent—maybe even be their real agent. People do that. And they'll all become huge successes, and it'll be thanks to you. "Gosh, if it weren't for Daniel . . ." they'll all say. Plus, in the short run, this is bound to smooth things over a little better between you and Graham. Delia will be pleased with you, too. This will really integrate you into their book.

And it's almost as if the author is saying, "Yes, Daniel. Yes, that's what I wanted," because right when you turn off the computer, the scratching stops.

THE BOOTH GETS more crowded, the conversation louder as the night advances. Jon was the last to arrive, so he's pulled up a chair at the end of the table. Monty sits beside you, and he's being particularly friendly to you tonight. Saturday is highball night at Lilly's, and the table is littered with empty glasses, abandoned slices of lime, and the stems of maraschino cherries. You want to tell Graham and Delia about your letter and the message you got from one of the concert halls this morning and the e-mail you received earlier in the week. It's going to be one of those "on the verge" scenes that Corrone talks about. On the verge of Graham's stardom. The moment Delia and Jon decide to follow suit. For hours, the announcement forms and reforms itself in your mind as you try to bring the subject around to music, but there's never a lull in conversation, and its flow is mysterious to you. It moves along on one topic, then suddenly dives into a hole and comes out behind you. It splits in two, then converges in the most unlikely places, then divides again, heading off into completely unexpected territory before returning quite naturally to answer a question that was posed forty minutes earlier.

Finally, you follow Graham into the men's room. It's not the ideal setting for the scene, but it's the first quiet moment you've had all night, and after the sound of flushing toilets dies down, you can hear for certain that the scratching has followed you. This is it.

Graham blows his nose. You wash your hands. Standing beside him at the sink, you catch his eyes in the mirror, and you say it. "Graham, I did something a little presumptuous," you begin, but that sounds all wrong, brings up uncomfortable memories. So you turn to face him—he's very tall up close—and you start again. "I was feeling creative a couple weeks ago . . ." But that doesn't sound quite right either. Didn't you have this dialogue all scripted in your head? But you can't remember what you planned, so now you pull a printout of the e-mail out of your pocket and hand it to Graham. His eyebrows rise as he begins to read.

"My agent?" he says.

"Uh-huh."

"Is this a joke?"

"No," you reply. "Seems like kind of good news, don't you think?"

"Seems like," Graham mumbles, still staring at the printout. It's from the symphony in Providence, Rhode Island. They're looking for a piano soloist for the summer series.

"And, um, I got a call, too," you say. "It's a small place up in Lowell. I can't remember the name, but they're auditioning new artists. Said they'd like you to send a CD of your work."

"A CD of my work," Graham laughs. "I'm very popular."

"I just did it, you know, on a lark," you tell him. "I figured since you're between jobs anyway, what better time, right? Are you angry?"

Graham's face opens up into a wide grin. "I'm not angry," he says. "That's the funniest thing I've ever heard! Come on." And he grabs your wrist and drags you back to the table. "Announcement! Announcement!" he shouts, interrupting a Jon story. "Guess which person at this table posed as my talent agent and got me invited on two auditions?"

"Are you serious?" Delia asks, her eyes darting from Graham to you.

You shrug, and Delia grabs the printout from Graham's hand.

"The Providence Symphony Orchestra!" Jon shouts, reading over her shoulder.

"Damn," Monty says. "What did you do?"

"Just sent a letter and a few reviews."

"Reviews?" Graham asks. "What reviews?"

Delia's eyes are wider than you have ever seen them. You've not felt so much attention from her since your first meeting one booth over. "From *Boston* magazine," you say. "*New England Jazz*, um . . . I can't remember. I wrote a few others."

"You wrote reviews?" Jon asks.

"Yeah."

"I guess it pays to have a fiction writer in the mix," Monty proclaims.

"I guess so," Graham says. "What did you say about me?"

"You can read them if you want," you say, fishing out copies of the letter and articles from the pocket of your jacket. "As you can see," you tell Graham with a smile, "you were universally admired." Graham reads through the small pile, chuckling periodically and tossing each page on the table as he finishes.

" '*Vibrant melodics*'?" Monty says, passing one of the articles to Jon.

"This is such a riot," Jon says. "So, do you bring Daniel to the auditions? Dress him all in tweed and horn-rim glasses like a real agent?"

"That would be cute," Graham says, "but it's not like I'm actually going to do them."

"What?" Delia asks.

This is not the reaction you expected.

"Are you kidding?" he says to her. "You know this isn't what I'm looking for right now. My sonata isn't finished, I don't have a damned CD, and hell, I don't even know what I'd audition with." In the silence that follows, he pulls a hand-rolled cigarette out of his shirt pocket, lights it, and coughs into the exhale. "Folks, I'm feeling like shit," he says, "so I'm going to take off for the evening. Daniel, thanks for the vote of confidence. And the laughs."

No one looks at anyone when Graham leaves. Delia stares down at the e-mail message, which sits in a small puddle on the table, Jon gathers the reviews into a pile, and Monty glances vaguely toward the door. "The letter was really ingenious," he tells you after a moment. "Wasted effort, though, I'm sure."

"No," Delia says, her voice subdued. "Graham doesn't feel well tonight. He'll appreciate it in the morning."

But he won't. You know it. You all know it. The author knows it, too. No one is looking at you, and you can feel yourself starting to sweat. Is the author trying to make you look bad? Stranger-comes-to-town-and-makes-an-ass-of-himself. That's what this feels like.

Graham

GRAHAM ARRANGES THE meeting on his cell phone during the quick walk from Lilly's to the Porter Square Station. The guy left a message for Graham a couple days ago—a new guy, must have been looking at an ad in one of the old papers. Though Graham wasn't planning to respond, for some reason he saved the message, and now he's glad he did. Where the hell did they get off? Acting like Daniel's pity and bullshit are just what Graham needs.

His anger subsides on the train ride over, and what thoughts remain of the scene at Lilly's he abandons at the Park Street Station, where he transfers to the Green Line. By the time he settles into a quiet corner at the Silent Owl, Graham has made himself nearly numb, save for a calm curiosity and the slightest twinge of guilt.

The idea first came to him a few months ago, after he'd been fired from Mick's Diner and the Olde Music Shoppe in rapid succession. He was having a drink at Jon's bar when his interest was roused by a series of classified ads on the back page of a gay newspaper: ads for companionship, escort services, and erotic massage. He asked Jon how people could advertise so blatantly, but Jon told Graham to look up "escort" in any phone book, and he'd find plenty of listings there, too. As long as the ad was discreet and the prostitute waited for the client to make the first move, the police weren't much of a threat. Graham didn't say anything else at the time, but the more he looked at help-wanted ads, the more tempting such lucrative and relatively effortless work seemed. So he talked it through with Delia and placed an ad: STRAIGHT COWBOY, 6'4", 23 YO.

Spotting his client walk in the door of the Silent Owl, Graham makes no motion to identify himself. He'll watch for a spell, see how the man carries himself. Graham has arranged fifteen meetings so far, and he has a screening process that he's perfected. As he did the first time, he asked the man what color necktie he would be wearing but offered no information about his own appearance. From a position of anonymity, Graham can look for any foreboding traits: too much ease or discomfort, foggy eyes, excessively poor health or grooming, any suggestion of a violent nature in the man's movements. Graham has rejected three men so far; the first appeared to be on some drug that made his body jitter.

Tonight's potential customer has salt-and-pepper hair and wears a tailored gray suit and a large, gold wedding band. He looks clean, relatively fit. Graham excavates his Texan drawl when the man passes his dark corner. "That's a mighty handsome blue tie," Graham says.

The man's composed expression lapses into surprise for only a second. "Well, hello," he says. "May I sit?"

Graham nods slowly. The guy has done this before.

"Can I offer you a drink?" the man says.

Graham glances at the cocktail in his hand.

"Well, maybe later." A long pause follows. "So . . ."

"Yeah, so . . ."

Maybe the man isn't so experienced, Graham thinks. The second man that Graham rejected refused to raise the subject within the ten minutes Graham allowed. Although he didn't honestly believe that the tiny man with asthma could be a plainclothes officer, Graham had no intention of taking any risks. Besides, he has no patience for nervousness.

"Well, I'm gonna have to take off in a few minutes," Graham tells the man.

"Oh, well, I hoped . . ."

"Yeah? Do you have something to say, boy?"

"Is two hundred dollars okay?"

"For . . . ?"

The man looks at the table and names a few tame sexual acts.

"Two fifty." It's always easy to add fifty. "And my mouth is off limits, but the rest is fine." The third time Graham walked away from a client, there was some disagreement over what Graham was willing to do.

On the way to the man's hotel room, Graham makes a show of calling his "agency" to let them know where he's going and when he expects to be back. He likes this part, feels like a kid playing cops and robbers. He's not sure if the men actually buy the performance, but it seems like a worthwhile precaution, and he takes some comfort in it.

The sexual acts themselves don't intimidate Graham. He's still young enough to find almost any sexual contact arousing, and he's never done anything but assume the dominant role, which makes matters fairly simple. Usually, he'll conjure other images to keep himself going, but there are times when Graham finds himself sufficiently stimulated by aspects of these encounters he doesn't like to acknowledge. For instance, when the salt-and-pepper-haired man lies down on his stomach and asks Graham to slap him a little, Graham does so with enthusiasm. And when Graham twists the man's arm behind his back, though he doesn't like to think about it, there is something satisfying about hearing the man whimper. And when Graham ventures to insult the man, which these married men sometimes enjoy, Graham can't help but notice a greater force to his own movements.

Graham's family background is not well known among his friends, and it's a warehouse of memories that he himself leaves locked and barricaded as much as possible. Grew up on a hog farm outside of Dallas—he's told them that. Doesn't speak to his parents or three brothers—that much he'll say before making it clear that the subject is not open for inquiry. Only Delia has been allowed a few glimpses inside that darkened warehouse where a lanky young Graham is pummeled with the byproducts of castrated hogs and tortured daily with accusations of homosexuality, which his brothers saw as the only explanation for a pianist living on a hog farm.

When Graham first stumbled into the music room at the age of eight, he had an ally in one of his brothers. Jimmy was just a year and a half older, and he would sing along when Graham played the piano at school or the keyboard at home. But when Jimmy turned twelve, he was taken under the wing of their two older brothers, who taught him to play football and basketball and to aim either at a person's head. Citing the similarity between the words "pianist" and "penis," the three pronounced Graham a "bona fide faggot" worthy of as much physical abuse as might escape the notice of a busy father and an indulgent mother. The greatest damage came from Jimmy, whose earlier camaraderie now required the public infliction of many bruises. Each session at the keyboard was interrupted by a smack in the head, a jab in the kidney, or the more painful sting of words. And Graham rarely fought back because whenever he challenged one brother, the attackers multiplied. So Graham played the piano, drank in the appreciation of his music teacher, ignored his parents as they ignored him, and waited to reach an age when he could leave Texas forever.

The departure came earlier than expected, when Jimmy, trying to force Graham to say "uncle," applied too much pressure to the thumb he was twisting. Graham heard the snap before he felt it. At sixteen, he'd been to the hospital before, but it felt different this time. He needed ten functional fingers to exist. Graham refused to speak to his brothers when they met him at the hospital and wouldn't even look at his parents. And when the cast came off six weeks later, Graham went from the doctor's office to the bus station without a bag or a moment's hesitation.

Thirty-seven dollars won't get a person from Dallas to Boston, where Graham's music teacher had said there were conservatories that would kill to teach someone with Graham's talent. Thirty-seven dollars gets a person from Dallas to New Orleans. That's something Graham only told Delia recently. A few months ago. At sixteen, Graham knew how to play the piano and how to breed and gut hogs. Neither did him much good those first two nights he passed wandering up and down Bourbon Street because people were there and awake and he had nowhere else to go.

The third night, he was still trying to figure out what to do when a short man with graying brown hair walked up and introduced himself. The guy was in his late fifties, a lawyer, well off, it seemed. He said Graham looked like he could use something to eat, so they went to a café, and the guy bought Graham a sandwich and a drink. They got to talking—about music, Boston, the hog farm—and it felt like Graham hadn't talked to another soul in his whole life. A few hours later, when the guy offered Graham three hundred dollars to spend the weekend with him, Graham felt ready to burst into tears. "Man, I'm not gay," he said.

"I didn't think you were," the guy said. "That's kind of the point. I figure, you need a plane ticket to Boston and a place to stay, and I've never been with a cowboy. What's the big deal?"

What *is* the big deal, Graham thought as he followed the man back to his hotel room. Just one more weekend to forget, one among many more unpleasant ones. What's the big deal, Graham told himself each time the man brought him to release. And if it was cathartic to be the one in control, to have someone begging him for a change, to pin someone else on the floor, well, what was the big deal? Graham never planned to think about the weekend again.

In Boston, Graham thought only of the future during the cab ride from the airport to the conservatory. And when the music director finally agreed to see him, Graham played the piano instead of answering questions. The music director arranged for him to stay with a couple of students, and the admissions office helped him get a GED, and the guidance counselor said Graham had shut out more memories than most men could in a lifetime. Which was exactly what he had intended to do. He didn't want to be one of those people who spends his life angry, plagued by a past that's best written off as a false start. So as a policy, Graham devotes almost as little thought to his life before Boston as he does conversation. But having found he can earn a week's pay in a forty-minute encounter and, at the same time, let off some of the steam from that barricaded warehouse without having to look into it, Graham doesn't long to abandon his current occupation any more than he wants to understand it.

Walking out of the salt-and-pepper-haired man's hotel room, Graham doesn't allow himself to think about the experience for even a minute. He doesn't think about Jimmy or Delia or Daniel or the auditions or reviews. He only permits himself to think about the sonata he's been composing. What's the big deal, he tells himself. This is easy money. This is what I'm doing so I can work in the morning.

This is not a big deal.

Don't even think about it.

Daniel

DELIA FINALLY CALLED you last night. After twelve days of misery. Twelve. You've hung out with them for five weeks in a row, but this past Friday and Saturday, you sat alone in your apartment all night, dressed, ready to go, if only the phone would ring or the scratching begin. But nothing. It was a long weekend. The only thing you didn't do was go to Lilly's— though you were torn, very torn. You just didn't want to risk humiliating yourself again, and you felt like someone should give you a call after that whole scene with Graham. Someone should smooth things over.

But no one called all weekend, and by Monday, you felt certain they were done with you—Delia and the author, too. Whatever this book was about, you'd fulfilled your role, you were becoming a nuisance. Or maybe the author was losing interest in everyone. Last night, when Delia called inviting you to lunch today, you felt dizzy with relief, but it wasn't until you walked into the restaurant a few minutes ago and heard the scratching sound greet you that you felt everything was going to be all right.

You're at a sandwich place near Boston University, not far from her office. This used to be a burger joint when you were in school; now, the walls are peach and white, and the menu emphasizes alfalfa sprouts. Delia arrives only a couple of minutes after you. She offers a friendly, gratuitous wave as she makes her way across the small room. "Thanks for coming," she says, giving you a quick hug before sitting down across from you. She smells like something floral and familiar. You haven't been alone with her since the night you two first met.

You study your menus and each other and exchange pleasantries about the train system and the weather. It's interesting to see her dressed for work. She still wears mostly black, white, and gray, but she looks more tucked in and pressed. Her lipstick is a little redder, her hair a hint more tame, her shoes a bit more formal. And she's wearing a blazer, fitted and flattering.

It's only after both of you have ordered that Delia folds her arms on the table and looks you in the eyes. "Look," she says, "I want you to know that I'm sorry about the way Graham reacted. That was a really nice thing you did. Not a lot of people do nice things for no reason."

"Oh, well, sure."

"I know Graham plays tough, but he's a delicate soul. I think his pride was hurt, but he does deserve those wonderful reviews you wrote. He's quite talented. Almost entirely self-trained before the conservatory." You nod at intervals that seem appropriate, and when the waitress arrives with two lattes, you both pause to add sweetener and stir. "Anyway,"

Delia continues after a minute, "I just wanted to thank you for what you did—even if it comes to nothing."

You say, "You're welcome," and take a sip of your drink, and when you put the mug down, Delia is smiling. "What?" you ask.

"You got foam all over your nose," she says, and she reaches over to wipe it off. For a moment, you and she both stare at the dollop of milk foam on her finger, and with an inward moan, you feel certain she is about to lick it off. But then the moment passes, and she is wiping her hand clean with a napkin. "Graham got a job," she says in a measured tone.

"Really? That's great."

"Well, it's not a *great* job, but it should bring in a little money. It's with this guy who does pet-sitting. He's overloaded, so Graham is helping him water plants and feed dogs now and then, just until the guy has things under control."

"That's good," you say. "It's something."

"Yes."

"Is he mad at me for the—"

"No," she says without looking up.

"No, I mean for before, for when we—"

"I know. No," she says again, now meeting your eyes. "That was bad of me. I've never done that before. But it was a mistake," she says. "Graham and I, we have our disagreements, but we're fine. Couples do that. They fight, they differ over little things and big things, they act out. Do you understand?"

Delia rests a hand on yours, and in spite of yourself, you're becoming aroused. Maybe the author won't notice. This is shameful because there's no sense spending the rest of the book longing for the girl you won't end up with. You'll just come off looking bad. Unless . . . maybe your night together was more than just Delia acting out. She's never done that before. Maybe she saw something in you that she won't admit. And a love triangle, the tension of it, makes for good fiction. Corrone has a whole section about it. He said half the reason his genocide novel got made into a movie was because of the thing between the diplomat's daughter, the school teacher, and the drug runner. In the end, of course, the girl always has to leave the guy who's clearly wrong for her and wind up with—

Don't allow yourself to think the words "Prince Charming." Not on the page.

"Daniel?"

"Yes?"

"Are you okay?"

And at that moment, the food arrives, and if you could kiss the author, you would, because salads are a great interruption. They require dressing and cutting and mixing, and you have to say, "Oh, doesn't that look beautiful? Oh, *yours* looks beautiful. Oh, it's delicious," and the subject is easily changed.

In this case, Delia picks up again with, "So, how's your book coming along?"

"Um, it's moving right along," you say. "I'm a few chapters in."

"What's happened so far?"

"Oh, guy meets girl and so on. Not the most original storyline, but there are complications."

"I'd love to read it one day," she says, picking a crouton off her salad.

"Not until it's done," you tell her.

"Fair enough."

"It may take a while," you add. Some writers take years to finish a novel.

"I'm a very patient girl."

The rest of the meal is more relaxed. She says they missed you last weekend, and she invites you to join them in the Fame

Game they've planned for Saturday. And it's a relief to feel back "in," even if your role is still a little unclear.

As you walk out of the restaurant, Delia apologizes again for Graham's reaction. "He's been going through . . . a difficult period," she says. "Actually, you have no idea what *perfect* timing this would be, if he'd just take advantage of it. It's exactly what he needs to turn things around."

And those words are a comfort to you, too. At least your instincts were right. You're still figuring out this whole book thing, but it's good to know that what you did for Graham and what you tried to do for Monty probably weren't the worst ideas you've ever had.

Monty

WHEN MONTY ARRIVES at Lilly's, Jon is in the middle of telling Graham and Delia a long story about something that happened last night at the bar where he works, so Monty sits and tries to be patient and tries to listen, but it all seems so trivial and irrelevant. The funny part, or what seems to be the funny part, comes when Jon has to forcibly evict a man from the bar, and when they all laugh, Delia smiles at Monty across the table, as if she's inviting him to share in the joke. So he smiles, tries not to be so serious. She has a way of bringing out the not-so-serious part of him. Always has.

He wants to burst out with his news, but now Graham is talking about his morning dog-walking adventure. He talks like he's a hero back from the war, like what he's doing is somehow noble. God forbid anyone mention the auditions he's passed up. Monty tried to say something to Delia about them the other day, but she changed the subject immediately, wouldn't even hear him out. She listens to Graham's story now and smiles at the right times, and it's even possible she still believes in him. It's possible. But what she needs to understand is that some people really do nothing with their lives. Even people with talent.

Of course, if she understood that, she wouldn't have dropped out of the conservatory the moment they tried to challenge her. Her mother would never have let that happen. Monty tried to talk Delia out of it, but alas . . .

He really would like to tell them his news. It's all so sudden. But now Jon is choreographing the next Fame Game, and that's always a complicated process. Monty agrees to play a director. Delia will be the movie star, as usual, and Jon and Graham will be her "people." And *Daniel*, it seems, will play a screenwriter. Monty thought Graham had frightened Daniel away, but apparently he'll be reappearing tomorrow night. What is it about Daniel Fischer from marketing that's so fascinating to people? Doesn't everyone in the marketing department have an amorphous novel in the works? Not that Monty has anything against the man, but Monty does prefer to keep his work life and personal life separate. It's a little uncomfortable bumping into him in the office cafeteria or at the occasional Bank Rome team meeting—but soon that won't be an issue.

"Okay," Monty says, unable to wait any longer, "I have an announcement to make."

He has interrupted something, but effectively, because even Jon stops talking and turns to him.

Monty takes a deep breath and says it. "I'm getting married."

"What?!"

"*Natalie*?" Delia says.

But that's not what he meant to say. The words surprise Monty more than they could anyone else. "No, I don't know," he says. "I mean, I *might* get married." Why did he say that? "Today, out of nowhere, I got offered this big promotion. I didn't even apply for anything. There's actually a hiring freeze," he tells them, "but my boss called me and said they need a new sales director in New York—"

"You're moving to *New York*?" Delia says.

"—and I just thought . . ." Monty's heart is racing. He can almost feel the blood pumping through his chest and down his arm and into his fingers. "I don't know," he says. "I haven't asked her, but I was just thinking as long as I'm going to be moving there . . ."

"That's terribly romantic," Graham says.

"I don't think that's quite how you should phrase the question," Jon agrees.

Graham goes to ask the bartender for a bottle of champagne—probably sparkling wine, this *is* Lilly's. Two booths down, a couple holds hands across the table as if they're—what, praying? Isn't it sacrilegious to say grace over bar food, Monty wonders. The talk around him is awkward. And meanwhile, the whole thing feels so much more real, now that he's said it. Of course he'll ask Natalie, tell her and then ask her. "It does make sense, right?" he says aloud. "This is earlier than I'd anticipated, but the job—that's earlier than I'd expected, too."

"Sure, it makes sense," Graham says.

"White picket fence," Delia mumbles.

Monty huffs. "More like a co-op on the Upper East Side."

"I can't believe you'd leave me," she says.

"Not immediately," he tells her, looking back into her narrow eyes. "It won't start for a couple of months."

It's hard to imagine being somewhere without Delia, and her eyes say the same thing. But Jon interrupts their silent exchange. "Exactly what happened?" he asks. "Your boss gave you a promotion, no interview or application?"

"Yes."

"During a hiring freeze?"

"It's wild," Monty says.

"It is."

The bartender arrives with the champagne, and Graham pours four glasses and laughs to himself. "So you need to talk to Natalie, boy."

"I do," Monty says. And he does. My God, he thinks, how is he sitting here like this? "I have to run, I'm sorry," he says. And walking out of the bar, he can picture it all—the wedding in his grandmother's house, the moving truck, the Manhattan apartment.

It's funny, Monty thinks. He always imagined he'd be the last of them to move to New York.

Jon

THE FAME GAME went so miserably that it was pure joy and candy when ten o'clock arrived and Jon was able to escape and head to work. It was kind of a shock when Daniel asked if he could tag along, but Lord knows, he was the only pleasant one all evening, so Jon said fine.

Jon is picking up abandoned glasses and cocktail napkins scattered about the Blue Lagoon, because that useless queen whose shift just ended is incapable of tidying up, while Daniel nurses a Lagoon Martini on one of the chrome stools that line the bar. Jon cast him as a screenwriter, quite naturally, and the poor boy is still wearing the red and black herringbone blazer and white jeans Jon selected for him. That black silk shirt might actually have been part of an old pajama set. It's hard to remember. At least he took off the beret. Jon, as usual, was Delia's dear-friend-and-entourage, and he spent dinner in a dangerous combination of Versace and imitation Versace. No human body has ever before been the receptacle for so many colors and patterns. Delia named the look "Medusa," and that witch was thrown into a duffel bag and replaced with jeans and a white T-shirt before Jon started his shift.

It really is a tragedy that they wasted the new fondue place on a night when no one was going to cooperate. First, Delia showed up at Jon's apartment in that bloodred taffeta number looking like a Spanish whore circa 1986. Hardly movie-star material. And Jon could have worked with that, except that she and Graham—her supposed Hollywood agent—were barely on speaking terms all night. Then Monty arrived a few minutes before Daniel and announced that precious Natalie had looked up Daniel's name and couldn't find his stories anywhere. Could he not he have chosen a slightly more tactful moment to share that little tidbit? Just the mention of Natalie's name threw Delia into a fit, which didn't make straightening her hair any easier. Jon burned his finger and nearly singed her ear—and she did have a point. Artists make up credits all the time, and Natalie can come on a little strong. But before Jon could decide whether to defend Daniel or side with Graham and Monty, the man walked in with a bottle of vodka and a goofy smile, and no one could look at him for half an hour.

The entrance at the restaurant went beautifully. They swooped through the doors wearing unnecessary sunglasses, and Daniel was so tickled when Jon delivered the ever-important opening line to the maître d'. "Look," Jon said, "I don't want *anyone* to make a big deal about her, but yes, that *is* Mimi Montgomery . . . the *actress*? And she just wants to have a normal dinner, okay? So no busboys asking for autographs, *capisce*?" The maître d' looked appropriately wowed, and within minutes, the waitstaff was whispering and staring. The night should have been brilliant.

But instead, it was excruciating. Jon had to start every conversation when the waiters popped up—and they were there all the time. It was fondue. That was the point. There's adjusting of burners and more napkins and more things to dip into pots and oh-don't-let-that-burn. But Monty seemed incapable of coming up with a fictitious cast for a fictitious movie, and Delia, who usually took no prodding to name an actress who looked fat in a swimsuit, just slathered Gruyère on everything and gave one-word answers. Jon had to drop every name, had to ask every leading question when someone came to refill their glasses. Graham's greatest contribution was to congratulate Delia for landing a part in a TV movie. It was a rather snippy thing to say, but it probably could have led to some amusement, if anyone had had the sense of humor for it. Daniel was the only one who tried all evening, but then he started that long story about meeting Victor Ramone's wife at the Oscars, when everybody knows the man isn't married. Yet another occasion for Jon to run damage control.

"Sorry tonight wasn't quite as much fun as usual," Jon says when he returns behind the bar.

"That's okay," Daniel replies, twirling his martini glass between two fingers. "Why are Delia and Graham fighting?"

"Oh, they're just going through a rough patch," Jon says with a sigh. "They'll be fine."

After a second, Daniel asks, "Did Graham have an affair?"

Jon turns on the sink behind the bar. "No," he says, keeping his back to Daniel.

"Does he deal drugs or something?"

"No, no. Definitely not."

"Then what?"

Jon doesn't want to go down this path. It's been a long night already. He fishes two glasses out of the sink and sets them on the drying rack. "They're getting past some things," he says, but Daniel looks unsatisfied. So Jon adds, "You might be familiar with one of those things, hmm?"

It takes a moment for this to sink in, but then the color rises in Daniel's freckled cheeks. His ears actually turn magenta. It's amazing.

"But," Jon continues, "like I said, they'll be fine. They always are. They're good together, they really are. You should have seen them in school and when they had their act. It was like they could read each other's minds."

"So why do you think Graham doesn't want to go on the auditions?" Daniel asks.

"Maybe he's not ready," Jon replies, returning to the sink. "I think he gets nervous being in front of other people. Truly performing. It's not the same as backing up Delia."

"Yeah," Daniel says quietly, and then, "Do you miss acting?"

Jon eyes Daniel through the mirror behind the bar. "No," he says. "It's not an easy life." Jon rinses out the martini shaker before a sigh escapes him and he turns back around. "You don't need to help me, Daniel. I'm the happiest person in this little group."

Daniel says nothing, but the color rises to his cheeks again.

"I hear Monty's getting a promotion," Jon adds.

"Is he?"

"How about that?"

Slowly, tentatively, Daniel nods.

"I like my life," Jon continues. "I have a fun job, don't work a lot of hours, meet amusing people. I'm doing what I want to do."

And the man who walks up to the other end of the bar seems to punctuate Jon's sentence: shaved head, polo shirt and jeans, thirties, maybe early forties. Jon moves down to greet him. Deep voice, nice features, simple rum-and-Coke man.

"Were you flirting with him?" Daniel asks when Jon returns.

"I think he's going to be my project for the evening," Jon says, winking across the bar. The man smiles. Cute dimples.

"You're not very subtle," Daniel says.

"Subtle is not always the best way," Jon replies, running a rag over the bar beside Daniel. "When I like someone," Jon continues, "I don't play games. I let him know." And with a deliberate lack of subtlety, Jon continues wiping the bar all the way to the other end.

JON CAN'T SLEEP, so he carefully pulls his arm out from beneath the figure beside him and steps out of the bed. The man from the bar shifts his legs and nuzzles the pillow but does not wake up. He's quite sexy, Jon thinks, pulling on a pair of boxers and walking into the bathroom. They had a nice time, and in the heat of the moment, Jon pictured a series of equally exciting sequels, but in the postcoital lucidity, he knows nothing could work out between him and Mark. Good cheekbones, a slim waist, and a powerful tongue cannot substitute for intelligence. Physical chemistry is not the only thing required.

Sexy and vapid, Jon thinks, glancing at his reflection in the mirror. That's what people probably think of him all the time, too. Not that Jon is vapid, but he can see how he might read that way. For a moment, he can't help admiring his own reflection: the large chest with a wisp of light hair at the sternum, the firm torso and broad shoulders. A lot of vain men in their thirties were skinny or chunky in their teens and twenties but not Jon. Sports came naturally to him, and the fact always showed. He didn't have to overcome horrible acne, didn't need to grow into his face. The same strong jaw-line that makes him look younger now made him look mature when he was in college.

Jon tosses a quick glance at the sleeping form in his bed. Maybe Mark . . . No, he thought Hefeweizen was a dictator. Graham will love that. Quietly, Jon slips out of the bedroom and moves to the kitchen to take an inventory of breakfast options. He can make omelets, pancakes—waffles are a pain. Has orange juice, coffee, cream. The chill from the refrigerator makes bumps rise on his arms, and Jon wraps himself in a cotton blanket as he settles into the brown leather chair in the living room.

He usually has no trouble sleeping with company, but it has been a taxing night. He and Daniel had a perfectly nice time in the end, but Jon's glad he said something about not wanting any help. What Daniel did for Graham was nice, but a little weird, and now this mysterious promotion for Monty. Not that Monty seems to suspect anything, but honestly, can't people put two and two together? Well, if Monty gets promoted and that makes him happy, then bully for him, but Jon had to tell Daniel not to get any bright ideas about resurrecting a buried acting career. What a nightmare it would be to audition again.

The resurgence of humiliation is not pleasant. Jon did get a handful of small parts, even an agent, without much trouble at all. It was fun. He met amusing people and thought he was building a career. At first, when his agent sent him on a couple of print modeling jobs, he agreed that it would be worthwhile to get his face out. And the money was an incentive, too. He didn't mind the first runway show, though he only did it as a favor when his agent said her usual guy backed out. But when he realized one day that he hadn't been on a stage in well over a year, that he was a regular feature in a growing pile of clothing catalogs, and that his appearance in *GQ* was probably the closest thing he'd get to a big break, Jon acknowledged the score. There is something to be said for knowing one's limitations.

After performing an Arthur Miller monologue for his acting class, which left him in tears and garnered the requisite applause from his classmates, Jon pulled his acting teacher aside and asked her for the truth. "If it's like I'm tone deaf, if I think I'm conveying something that I'm not, you'll be doing me a favor by telling me. Am I ever going to play anything other than Pretty Man Number Two?" And the teacher didn't say no, but she didn't have to. They went out for coffee and talked it over. It was okay to do some modeling if it was supporting a fledgling acting career, but if this was all he was going to have, if he was never going to be in a play in any significant capacity, he'd rather read plays and see plays and do something different with his time in this world.

Yes, Jon muses, pulling his knees up under the blanket, it was a good decision. So many people waste their lives pursuing dreams that are never going to come true for one reason or another. And what if he *did* spend years in acting classes and land a few decent parts in local productions? That's all it could ever amount to. There would be a whole lot of labor, a whole lot of rejection. Friends saying they saw his picture in the latest J. Crew catalog. And on his deathbed, what would he be able to say for himself? I played an adequate but unremarkable Biff Loman and facilitated the sale of lots of chinos and mock turtlenecks.

Leave ambition to Daniel and Monty. And if Daniel inspires Graham and Delia to get their acts together, good for them. They at least have talents worth cultivating. And honestly, Jon thinks, as he has thought before, they should really commit themselves one way or another. Either be happy pursuing music or be happy not. But why be miserable about artistic failure when you aren't pursuing artistic success?

Jon shuffles back into the bedroom. Mark looks as adorable as before, and when Jon slides into bed, the warmth of Mark's skin against his own is arousing. He kisses Mark's shoulder, then his neck, then his prickly shaved head. And when Mark smiles half-consciously and returns the kiss on his lips, the sequel begins.

Daniel

MONTY'S APARTMENT IS not quite what you imagined it would be. You somehow pictured it with wood paneling and lots of antique furniture, but the black leather sofa is square with no arms and the glass coffee table very modern in its simple design and brushed silver frame. Everything in the room, from the bookshelves to the lamps, is either black or silver, with the exception of the exposed brick on two walls and a very large painting on one of the two black walls. An original painting, not a print. Something abstract with thick blue paint-swirls that stick out from the canvas by at least half an inch. A baby grand piano sits in the far corner of the room. Graham is hovering near it.

"Going to play something new for us tonight?" Monty asks as he hands Graham a martini.

Graham steps back, his eyes still on the piano, and nods.

"World premiere," he says, and then he catches your eye and gives you a wink.

"And Daniel, I hope you brought something to read," Monty continues. "Natalie is going to read some poetry, but I assured her she wouldn't be the only writer here this evening."

"Sure," you say as you cough past a tickle in your throat. "Of course."

Delia beams at you. "I can't wait!" she says.

"Me neither," Monty says to her.

When Delia called you earlier in the week to invite you to Monty's engagement-slash-promotion party, you initially felt nothing but relief. She kind of ignored you last weekend during the Fame Game dinner, and that conversation with Jon made you feel even more like you were losing your footing in the book. But her voice sounded so sincere over the phone. She apologized for being "off" the other night and complimented you for putting on a good show as the group's screenwriter. And when she told you about Monty's party—a "salon night," she called it—where she'd be singing and Graham playing, she was so cute and nervous about asking you to read something that you agreed without thinking.

"They just asked him out of nowhere," Natalie is saying. "During a *hiring freeze*. Can you believe it?"

"That is extraordinary," Jon replies, with a quick glance toward you.

You edge away from them and, turning, splash a few drops of Chianti onto your hand and shirt. No one sees you or says anything, so you slip into the bathroom to wash your hands, wet the stain, and escape. You were smart enough to keep your mouth shut this time, and even if Jon is suspicious, he doesn't seem to have said anything. It's not like you got Monty the job. You just happened to be a few tables away from his boss one day at lunch when Monty was mentioned as one of a handful of people being considered for this promotion. So you started a rumor about him leaving to join another firm, made sure the rumor got to his boss's secretary. It was almost effortless. At twenty-eight, Monty's pretty young to be getting a director-level job, but he dreams of early retirement, so now he's more clearly on the fast track. At least someone's life will change for the better in this book, and maybe the reader knows you had a hand in moving things along.

You run a wet hand-towel over the sleeve of your shirt—which is going to stain, no question—and when you turn off the faucet, you hear a familiar scratching in the air. The final guest has arrived. It's hardly a surprise, given what's coming up. But you're not thinking about the performance you're going to have to give. A part of you is working very hard not to think about it.

At first, you didn't think it would be that difficult to write a story for salon night. You've read enough novels, been in a few. And all the plotting you had to do to get Graham those auditions and to help Monty, it's not unlike what an author has to do. So you reread Corrone's advice about story structure and fictional truth and planting seeds and all that stuff, and you sat down at your computer, but that's where the trouble came. The blank computer screen was so . . . blank. You started to write a story about a detective, which you abandoned and replaced with a story about a gambler, which you abandoned and replaced with a story about nothing at all, which you abandoned and replaced with half a bottle of merlot and an invocation to the author. That didn't go so smashingly either. Just a sad man alone in his apartment on his knees crying. Not pretty. You're glad the author didn't show up to record that scene.

Does the author want to see you succeed or fail this evening? You're not sure, but you're already a little nauseated, and you can feel your brow beading up with sweat. You run the wet towel over your forehead, take a deep breath. Wine and brie on an empty stomach—not a good idea.

When you step out of the bathroom, Natalie is passing from the kitchen with a new bottle of wine, and she stops to top off your glass. The light catches her ring, and you congratulate her once again. "It was his great-grandmother's," she tells you, as he told you before. You offer a prolonged "ohhh" or something like that, trying to sound interested, but not so interested that she'll say any more about it.

Across the room, Delia and Graham are laughing with Monty and Jon, reminiscing about old recitals and shows. Everyone seems to be getting along again, which is a relief, though part of you didn't mind knowing that Delia and Graham were fighting. Tonight, she's all smiles and good humor. She keeps grabbing Graham's hands and tussling his hair. She gave you an enormous hug when you walked in the door. She's even being polite to Natalie. She congratulated her earlier, and now she's complimenting her on her dress.

At last, Monty offers a few corny words of thanks and welcome, and the show begins. He goes first, sitting down at the piano and launching into a waltz. Almost immediately, Jon and Natalie begin to dance in the center of the room, which appears to have been cleared for that purpose. His movements aren't clumsy or awkward, and you imagine yourself following suit. You'd walk up to Delia, take her hand. You'd lead her onto the floor—which is considerably more spacious in your mind—and you wouldn't step on her toe once. You'd be graceful, and she'd follow your lead. Your heart would not be pounding. No, you'd be calm. Her hand would squeeze your shoulder, and—

Her hand actually is squeezing your shoulder. "I'm looking forward to hearing you read tonight," she says.

"Oh," you say, which of course is not the right response. "Well, I'm looking forward to hearing you sing."

"Are you reading from your book?"

"No," you say. "I brought a story. I hope you like it."

"I'm sure you'll be incredible," she says. She's wearing a short black dress with dramatic folds down the front, and around her neck is a black choker. Natalie, with the lace on her sleeves and a yellow ribbon in her hair, looks like a schoolgirl by comparison.

"You, too," you say. "Incredible."

After Monty finishes the second waltz, you all take seats around the coffee table while Natalie reads a lengthy poem about spring and loneliness and green leaves and waterfalls. For the first time all evening, the energy drains from Delia's face. She looks distracted, bored. And in her defense, you decide that this must be a bad poem. Not that you read a lot of poetry, but this feels bad. You wonder if Graham will roll his eyes like that during your reading, if Jon will keep crinkling the napkin in his hand. Natalie reads another poem—this one shorter—and then another long piece about a girl and her mother and magazine models and menstruation. And during the polite applause that follows, you slip into the kitchen and refill your wineglass to the rim.

Natalie is sitting in your chair when you return to the living room, so you take Graham's place on the sofa beside Delia. She gives you a friendly smile, then directs her attention to the piano, where Graham sits, his sport coat crumpled up on the floor beneath him. He ignores her, ignores all of you. He studies the keyboard, releases a deep breath, then launches into a piece that moves so quickly it makes you dizzy to watch his fingers. No napkin-crinkling or glassy stares now. Even you lose yourself in the music, in the sight of Graham's long arms crossing the keyboard. In spite of yourself, you feel just a hint of awe, and when you look at Delia, you can see, with disappointment but without surprise, that she is filled with a far greater awe, her lips not smiling or frowning but opened as if to drink the music in. That's the look you want. Let her feel that way when you're up there.

And minutes later, you are up there. Standing before the fire-place, straightening and shuffling the pages of your story, clearing your throat, surveying in agony the five pairs of eyes that watch you expectantly, listening to the sound of the scratching pencil, which feels like a mockery after the music that filled the room. For a moment, you have an image of the author, feet propped up on a desk, scribbling and smirking down at you, waiting for you to fail. Then Natalie interrupts your fantasy, asks if you want a glass of water, and you say yes, so she goes to get it and you all wait. Graham is smoking furiously before an open window. Monty strokes his goatee. Jon spreads cheese onto a cracker. Delia makes her hand into a little fist and offers you a silent cheer.

She's looking forward to hearing your story. *Your* story. Well, fine. It's not bad. It really isn't. You solved the problem this morning when you flipped to the Corrone chapter called "Every Story Has Already Been Written." It wasn't the sentiment of the chapter that helped you, but the idea that popped into your head. So you went on to the Internet, found a satisfactory story, reformatted it on your computer, and printed it out. Obscure author—you checked—and the man has no published books, no impressive magazine credits. It wasn't even a good website. Not one you've ever heard of. This is going to be fine. They'll all be impressed. It seems like a good story.

And a moment later, glass of water by your side, you're reading. It's a story about these two contortionists who work in the circus. And they're getting older, and one of them is afraid he has arthritis, so it's kind of sad. But it's also funny, you realize, when the group chuckles for the first time. The business about the unemployed clowns. You didn't notice before. And when you glance up between pages, you see admiration in everyone's eyes and undeniable pleasure in Delia's. The story feels longer than you expected, but you're enjoying it a whole lot more tonight than you did this morning, and when you look up at the end, you can see a hint of awe in Delia's eyes as well. Just five people, but their applause is rich and satisfying, and you feel a pride of creation you've never known before.

"Was that one of your published stories?" Natalie asks in the blur of compliments.

Better to say no, you decide. This one is new.

"I loved it," she adds. "Where were you published again?"

"Oh, it's been a while," you say. "*Wisconsin Review*."

"And wasn't there another one?"

"Um . . . *Lavender Dream*."

"Right," she says, squeezing your hand. "Well, great job."

And Delia says it, too. Says that your story is wonderful, that she loves it. And when she hugs you, she holds on for a second longer than necessary.

But a moment later, she's gone, standing beside the piano. Graham has put on his sport coat again, and they whisper to each other before he takes a seat at the bench. Then she nods back at him, he launches into a jazzy vamp, and suddenly Delia's voice fills the room. She's singing "It Ain't Necessarily So." It's a Gershwin song, and you've heard it before, but not the way she sings it. Her voice is sultry, rich, a little husky. You melt into the sofa. Her composure is intoxicating. No hint of nervousness, none of the self-consciousness of Natalie's reading. She doesn't close herself off like Graham. She looks each of you in

being written

the eye—Jon, Monty, you, even Natalie. She sings to each of you.

It's such a revelation to see someone in her element for the first time. *This* is who she is. She said it herself the night you two met. *This* is what she should be doing. She has the talent, the looks, the charm. She's just gotten sidetracked, run into obstacles. All she needs now is a push. And that's where you come in—of course. Graham, Monty, Jon, her family, they've had years to help her out. Now it's up to you. This could totally be a book about her rise to success. Meeting you is going to change her life.

Your heart is racing, and when the song ends, you, Jon, Monty, and Natalie jump to your feet with applause. There's no thinking involved. You feel propelled upward. In a flash, you picture Delia singing in a huge auditorium before hundreds of people. And a chill passes over you, because the image is so vivid that you're almost certain it's not a fantasy but a premonition.

Delia

THE CAR IS filling up with the stale, suffocating smell of those goddamned cigarettes he insists on rolling like he's some kind of rock star. "Would you please try to hold it outside?" Delia tells him for the second time. Graham adjusts his arm without saying anything. Most of the smoke rushes out the window, but she still has to combat the smoke that has already clouded up the inside of the tiny Corolla. She turns on the air conditioner.

"That's just going to recirculate the smoke," he tells her.

"It'll clean some of it out."

"Fine," he says.

It's Saturday evening, and they're driving back from her father's house in Winchester. They went around five this afternoon to water the plants and check the mail. Her father is in China on business—probably beating the children in the sweatshops, Delia muses—and Graham insisted on going with her, which was annoying, because he always complains about it, plus they tend to fight when they're in the car for too long. Still, she's got to bring it up. They started the conversation. The bills are one thing, but—

"I thought this pet-sitting thing was a paid job," she says before she can frame the discussion in her mind.

"It is. I told you."

"Well, the rent is due next week. I can't cover that, too, so you need to ask him to pay you."

"He will."

Delia stares out the window at the row of tenement houses along Mystic Avenue. They've been driving for twenty minutes and have said very little since she mentioned the power bill in what was intended to be a nonchalant way. "I'm just worried," she says at length, her voice cracking at the end.

"I'll have the money by next week," he tells her. "It'll be fine."

"And what about when this is over?" she asks, turning to face his rigid profile. "Graham, you need to get a real job."

"This *is* a job."

"If you think it's going to be steady . . . then that's great."

"I've got things under control."

They sit in silence for a minute or two, and when he tosses his cigarette butt out the window, she turns back to him. It has to be said. "I can't ask my father for any more money."

"To support your 'deadbeat husband'?"

"That's not what I said."

"But it's what you meant."

"No," she says, pressing her head back against the ripped vinyl headrest, "but I do have an income. If it were just me, I wouldn't have to ask him for money."

"I get it. Well, I'll have the rent, and I can pay you back for some of June, too."

"Then it's fine," she says, staring at the yellow dashes ahead of them. He's speeding now. Like they're in a rush. Well, it'll be nice to get out of the car, maybe take a long bath before heading to Lilly's. Maybe she'll call Giorgio, schedule a massage for tomorrow or the next day. There's still money on the gift card from Christmas, and her neck feels so tight, her back, all over. She tries to imagine the feeling of his hands untying her muscles.

"But why does it matter anyway?" Graham asks when they hit the next red light. Giorgio disappears. "Your dad's loaded. You're his kid. Why is it such an ordeal?"

"I'm an adult," she says, facing his stare. "And so are you. We should be able to take care of ourselves. Graham, is your friend not going to pay you?"

"I *said* he's going to pay me. This is a side note. I never understand why you get so upset asking the man for money every once in a while."

"The light is green," she tells him.

Graham shifts gears and turns back to the road. For at least a minute, Delia watches the hubcaps spin on the car beside them. Then she asks, "Why don't you ask your parents for money? Think that'll be fun?"

"You know that's different. You talk to the man every day. Shouldn't you get some compensation?"

"I do not talk to him every day, thank you very much. And he's my father, not my bank account."

"He's a dick, that's what he is. You say so yourself all the time."

"Yeah, he is a dick. But has it ever occurred to you that every time I ask for money, I feel more obligated to him?"

"Yes, it has," Graham says, digging another cigarette out of his shirt pocket. "I'm just not sure you'd act any differently without that sense of obligation."

"Oh, what's that supposed to mean?"

"Nothing," he replies, raising a lighter to his cigarette. The exhaled smoke fills the car again.

"Graham!" she says.

"Sorry," he mumbles, rolling down the window. "It's just that you work at the job he got you, you water his fucking ferns whenever he goes out of town—you know, a man who travels for months at a time really should not have ferns. It's very inconsiderate."

"Is that your professional plant-waterer opinion?"

Graham shrugs and takes a long drag.

"So I suppose I should kill the ferns and get myself fired. Would that be your advice?"

"I don't know what you should do," he says.

"Well, what are *you* doing? And why won't you go on the auditions Daniel set up? I don't get it."

"No, you don't, do you?"

"No," she says, switching the air conditioner to high. "He practically laid a music career at your feet. It was very thoughtful of him. If you're such a devoted musician—"

"Yeah, that was pretty thoughtful, wasn't it? He wrote that shit without ever hearing me play a note. Should I be flattered?"

"Who cares? Why shouldn't he have assumed you're good? And why shouldn't you go for the auditions? They could be your break, your chance to make money from music instead of—"

"Daniel didn't get me shit," Graham says. "I could get my own auditions. I could get real letters of introduction from people who know a thing about music. Doing it later on my own is no different from doing it now in gratitude to your little Daniel."

"Doing it now means doing it," she mutters. "Later with you seems to mean never."

"Right back at you," he tells her, taking another long drag. "*You've* got a pretty stellar music career going for you. Get any big breaks at the Methodist Home?"

Delia can feel the anger rising to her cheeks. "Fuck off."

"Art's a funny thing," he tells her.

"Well, I take what I can get."

"You take what you can fit into your lunch break," Graham snarls. "You think I'm not trying? I've written two new pieces in the last six months, and I've almost got a handle on the Rachmaninoff. What do you sing for them? 'Over the Fucking Rainbow'?"

"Well, maybe I need to start whoring myself out so I can have a little more free time. That would be a very high-minded thing to do."

Graham turns the car onto their street and shrugs. "You could just whore yourself out for the fun of it," he says. "Isn't that more your style?"

Daniel

YOU'VE STARTED KEEPING the apartment somewhat tidy
on account of the watchful eyes of the author, but you still
weren't prepared for Delia's phone call. She's coming over instead of meeting everyone at Lilly's. Sounded upset. Was she
crying? You're not sure, the conversation was so brief. And
now, as you survey the living room through her eyes, the author's scratching pencil accompanying the racing of your pulse,
you wish you could replace the Monet print above your sofa.
You wish you had more modern furniture, a more eccentric
decor. You pick up the magazines and envelopes that litter the
kitchen table. You sniff the sheets in the bedroom, hoping the
author doesn't see. They're fine. Wipe up the mildew spot beneath the soap dish in the bathroom.

What else will she notice? You rest a Nabokov novel promi-
nently on the night table, then change your mind and tuck it

away on the bookshelf. You haven't gotten past the introduction. She might ask. You leave the Corrone manual on the desk in the living room but put away his novel with a twinge of guilt. It's not exactly highbrow. You flip through your CD collection, put a few jazz and classical discs in the front of the rack. You change into a more flattering pair of jeans and a polo shirt. Spray cologne on your neck, chest, then neck again. You check the clock: nine thirty. Then you change underwear, do thirty sit-ups, and dress again—same jeans, tighter shirt. You adjust your hair. Is the cologne too strong? You take off your running shoes and search the bedroom for a missing brown shoe, but then the doorbell rings and you answer it in a pair of white socks.

Delia hugs you at once. There's a smear of eye shadow on her cheek, but otherwise, she wears no makeup. At first, she says nothing but thank you; then she collapses onto your sofa without even a glance at the Monet print. You sit beside her, and she slides over to lean on your chest. You can feel her breath rising and falling, and carefully, you wrap your arm around her and rub her back as she begins to cry. You imagine yourself leaning down to kiss her neck, the spot behind her ears. You wonder how she'd react. Perhaps she'd lift her head to face you, letting you kiss her eyelids, her nose, and then her lips. They'd taste sweet, like pink cocktails.

"Thanks for letting me come over," she says with a sniffle.

Your face is hot and undoubtedly red, but she's not looking at you.

"No problem," you manage. You crack your neck, clear the tickling sensation from your throat. "So, can I get you something to drink?"

"That would be great," she says, sitting up to face you. "Wine, if you have any."

You worry for a moment that you have nothing but soda and

juice, then remember the box your parents sent from their recent Mediterranean cruise. That was convenient—at the very least. "We're in luck," you tell her, pulling the box out from the bottom of the pantry. "We have an entire continent at our disposal. Sangiovese, Bordeaux . . . ?" Delia smiles for the first time as you line up the bottles on the bar between the kitchen and the living room.

She selects a Spanish table wine, you open the bottle, and the two of you settle back onto the sofa, where Delia tells you about a fight she just had with Graham. Once she starts talking, it's like she can't stop. He criticized her for helping her father, for keeping her job, for not singing enough. He was cruel. He was unreasonable. You pour her a second glass, which she downs almost instantly. She wants to spend more time singing, she says. She wants to move to New York. That was always the plan. But it's not like they have the money, and in the meantime, what else is she supposed to do? Do what he did? "Oh, I shouldn't say this," she says. "I shouldn't, but when you and I first met . . ." She's sniffling, and you run to the bathroom to grab her a tissue, but the box is empty, so you pull off a long strip from the toilet-paper roll and hand it to her. ". . . Graham was . . ." She hesitates again, you wipe a tear off her cheek with the other end of the toilet-paper strip, and then she tells you that Graham was working for a few months as a hustler. For men.

The scratching of the pencil is almost frantic, and for the next minute or two, it's difficult to concentrate on anything she says. You struggle to maintain a facial expression that suggests both that Delia was right to let Graham try it out—"Yes, he should've realized immediately . . ."—and was right to be horrified—"Of course, you couldn't live like that." And no, you say, you're not mad at her for using you to make her point. "I'm glad to have met you," you say. The words sound rigid and flat.

Meanwhile, what's whirling around in your head is *wow-oh-my-god-this-is-incredible*. And yet it all makes sense when you think back on it—that morning when Graham came in, the way they acted toward each other—yes—their fighting, their making up, his quitting his "job." What a moment in the book, and to be here with Delia as the reader finds out that this major character isn't who he seems to be—

Unless the reader has known all along.

That would suck.

There's a pause in her speech. You're not sure where she left off. You desperately want to tell her that she's too good for Graham, but that seems like a risky thing to say. She came to you for support. For comfort. And what's more, you have a job to do if you're going to be the one who sets her on the path to stardom. So you tell her she was brilliant at Monty's party, that you knew she'd be good, but you couldn't have imagined how powerful her performance would be, that you've never heard a better singer. "I had a vision of you on a big stage with a huge audience," you tell her. "You could really be something."

Delia pushes you away mockingly, and her hand against your chest sends a surge through your entire body.

"I'm serious," you say.

"I wish I could give it a go," she tells you, "at least try, but it's not that easy. Graham clearly doesn't understand the concept of planning. And my father was so horrible the one time I asked him for help. He said I could never make it in New York, that I'd be crushed, the way everyone else is. He's happy to buy me a pair of shoes or pay for a haircut, but he won't do anything that truly helps. It's true, he has no faith in me, like Graham always says. And now with Graham hardly working, it's impossible to save anything, and the move keeps getting pushed further and further away. And he's right, what am I doing with my life in the meantime? It's just not fair."

You lose yourself for a moment in Delia's eyes, black and brilliant from recent tears. "No, it's not fair," you say, gently caressing her shoulders. Not fair at all, you think. Not fair that people who deserve to be in the spotlight are so easy to over-look. Not fair that people stay with lovers who are wrong for them. Not fair that Graham can cheat on her and mooch off her and sit at home all day, delaying her dreams, obstructing them. Not fair that she loves him anyway, that you can't insist she leave him at once. That she's telling you what a good friend you are and doesn't seem to consider you as possibly more, and if you tell her how you feel about her, you may jeopardize any relationship with her at all, to say nothing of your place in the book. *Her* book, which isn't fair, since being in a book is *your* dream and not hers. It's not fair that the author has probably recorded this argument between Graham and Delia, that it may have made for good reading, that their relationship continues to usurp any hint of a romantic storyline involving you, and that your best hope for staying in this book is in the role of support-ive friend and yes-man. There is so much that is unfair about this moment. And when Delia asks if she can spend the night on your sofa, it feels like perhaps the most unfair moment of all.

You say yes. You toss her purse onto the chair, get sheets and a blanket from the linen closet, a pillow from the bed. "Tell me everything will be okay in the morning," she says when you finish making up the sofa. She is five years younger than you, and for the first time since you met her, she really seems it.

"I'm sure it will," you say.

The scratching stops as you cross the threshold of your bedroom and returns the next morning as you pass through it again. The blanket is neatly folded in the center of the sofa, and on it sits a note, thanking you for listening to her silly problems and asking you not to say anything to Graham or "the boys." She's gone home to make up with him. She just needs to be patient, she writes, and everything will work itself out. See you soon. Hugs and kisses.

Hugs and kisses. On paper. That's what you get.

"What the hell . . . ?" you say to yourself, to the note, to the author. "Why are you even *here* if this is all I get?"

Of course the author says nothing.

You fall onto the sofa beside the blanket. Your head aches and you're tired. You're not sure what you're supposed to do. "What are you writing about me?" you ask.

And you can see it coming like a slap in the face. No response. No sign. And the scratching stops.

THE AUTHOR'S PENCIL greets you in your apartment as soon as you return from the gym. You've been waiting all day for something to happen—some idea to come to you, some sign. Around lunchtime, you thought you heard the pencil scratching outside, so you jumped into the shower, dressed, and got ready for whatever might come next. But then you realized it was just the neighbor's lawnmower you were hearing and felt pretty stupid. The same clean blue shirt you put on this afternoon hangs from your closet doorknob. You actually ironed it this afternoon while you were waiting for . . . what? Nothing, as it turned out.

At the moment, you're wearing running shorts and a T-shirt, both drenched. You spent a good forty-five minutes on the treadmill trying not to think about Delia's note to you this morning. You're sweaty. You're overheated. You smell bad. You don't feel like you should spend much time on the page in this condition, but you wait a moment to see if the author's intentions will become apparent.

You get a bottle of water from the kitchen. Drink it. Five minutes pass. You drink a second bottle. Ten minutes. You take a shower. Pencil still scratching away. You eye the blue shirt. It's a little dressy for a Sunday night at home. Is nothing going to happen, you wonder. Corrone says that sometimes it's important just to observe the characters, and that may be important, but it's damned uncomfortable for the characters. You can't very well spend a whole chapter watching television and paying bills. The author must have a reason for viewing this moment in your life as significant.

That's when you notice your cell phone blinking: Delia. But you barely have time to get excited because the message is as infuriating as the note. No reference to your conversation last night or her early departure this morning. She wants to know if a set of keys slipped out of her purse in your apartment. They're her father's house keys, not her own, so she doesn't need them immediately. She just wants to know if they're there.

You go to the chair where her purse was last night and find the keys half-hidden behind a throw pillow. Pretty anticlimactic, if this is all the author wanted to show. You worry for a moment that you're going to sound annoyed if you call her back right away—because you are annoyed, with her, with the author—but then it also occurs to you, as you set the keys down on your coffee table, that maybe you should infer something from their presence. The author's goal is probably not exclusively to piss you off.

The pencil continues to scratch. Keys. Father. The scratching intensifies, and you're trying to think, but you wish the sound would go away for a few minutes. With the author's presence always comes a sense of expectation, and it's a lot of pressure thinking on the spot like this. You never let them push you to give off-the-cuff ideas at the office; you always ask for time to reflect, to think things through. You walk from the living room to your bedroom and back. Her father's out of the country, and she's stopped by to check on the house a few times over the past couple weeks. Is that supposed to be helpful?

The scratching still won't go away, so you decide that you will. You put on a new T-shirt and a clean pair of running shorts and head outside. At the corner, you turn left. But the scratching follows you even when you quicken your pace. Down Lawson Street, onto Greer, through that little playground. You're running pretty fast now, but you can't shake the author, and all the while you're trying to make sense of this sign. You must be on to something here. Keys, her father's house, last night, Graham, her money problems—

And that's it. You're crossing over Brookside, author close by, when you figure it out. That house is empty. Mr. Benson goes away for months at a time. What Delia should do is take her late mother's jewelry. She's complained about how her father won't let her touch any of it for fear she'll sell it. But of course, that jewelry is rightfully hers, and like she said, if it's worth enough to give her a start, why not sell it? "The Freedom of the Brooch": it doesn't have to be a play, it could be real. Or the title of a book, maybe *this* book.

This could actually solve everything. If Delia didn't feel so tied down, she could quit her job, focus on her music, and make her dreams happen. She'd be free to move to New York, and that's an easy train ride away. She'd have an excuse to get away from Graham, and with distance, she'd realize she needs to disentangle herself from him once and for all. In fact, without her to support him, Graham would probably start hustling again, and then she'd be sure to drop him.

This is perfect. Monty's moving to New York, so he's bound to back you up on the idea, and depending on how long her father's away, Delia could be safely settled in New York by the time he's back. You jump a recycling bin like it's a hurdle. All you have to do now is convince her to do it, "and I'm not going to try to do that over the phone," you say aloud. "All right?" You turn right at the corner and head toward the traffic light at Comm. Ave. Your heart is pounding. You check your watch. You can probably make it to the corner in less than ten seconds. "All right?" you say again. The author's pencil seems to slow down, and when you reach the intersection nine seconds later, the scratching vanishes into the sounds of the traffic.

YOU'RE STANDING ALONE in a darkened bedroom, for a moment too mesmerized by the pink comforter with lace trim and the tiny flowers in the wallpaper to notice that the scratching sound has returned. You scan the tiny ballerina figurines on the white bookshelves built into the wall, then stop when you hear it. It's after nine o'clock in the evening, and you're surprised that the scratching didn't greet you earlier. In fact, moments ago, you considered calling the whole thing off if the author didn't arrive soon. With a nod of greeting, you walk out of Delia's childhood bedroom to find her father's room.

When you woke up this morning, you realized that yesterday's brilliant idea wasn't without its flaws. Delia isn't going to stand up to her father the way you think she should. She needs help. That's what you've thought all along. That's why you're in this book. So you revised your plan, looked up her dad on the Internet, waited until dark, then headed to the empty house in Winchester.

You pass several doors along the upstairs hallway and head

for the last room, which has mahogany furniture and a faint, musky smell. Her father's bedroom is as neat and organized as the rest of the house. You shine your penlight into the closet. Clothes are folded and lined up on the shelves. No piles or boxes litter the floor. Carefully, you reach between the folded stacks of sweaters and golf shirts to see if there's anything hidden behind them. You're wearing a pair of yellow plastic gloves, the kind your mother would wear to wash dishes or clean the bathroom, but you don't feel like a burglar. You have the keys, and you're here on Delia's behalf.

All you're going to do is take the jewelry. That way, she never has to claim responsibility for it and won't have to fight with her father. You just want to make this as easy as possible for her. If you make the house look like it's been burglarized and pawn whichever pieces she tells you to, she could have the cash in hand long before her father has a chance to report any "crime." And if she hates the idea of selling the jewelry—but why would she?—she can just put everything back in the house before her father returns.

You shine your light under the bed—nothing but dust and bed slippers—but as you rise to your feet, you pause at the night table. There's a small framed picture of a little girl wearing a pink and white bathrobe and holding a microphone that's bigger than her arm. She's about seven years old, with dark, wavy hair that falls below her shoulders and a familiar mischievous look in her eyes. Destined for the stage, you think. Did the author put that there for you to see? Thanks, you want to say. You say the word in your head.

It was strange that the author took so long to arrive. You were alone when you started the rumor that got Monty his promotion, but that was office chat. A break-in seems like it would be worth recording. When you slid the key in the side door and still heard no scratching, you started to wonder whether this was something the author didn't want you to do. Maybe the forgotten keys were supposed to be a sign for you to do something different. Or maybe they weren't a sign at all but merely a forgotten set of keys.

Now, as you begin a slow search through the dresser drawers, you are feeling hopeful. The scratching of the author's pencil moves in tandem with your heavy breathing, and these sounds, coupled with the opening and closing of drawers, echo through the dark bedroom. The contents of the drawers are unremarkable: socks, old wallets and watches, handkerchiefs, cologne. But in the back of the bottom drawer, you find a blue velvet box which you open to discover, without surprise, the jewelry you've heard so much about.

"Are these real?" you mumble aloud. The pieces are cumbersome in size and setting. They look like the kind of costume jewelry you see in movies or at discount department stores, only they're surprisingly heavy. There are several rings with large, colored stones surrounded by small diamonds. There's a pearl necklace, which Delia once said would be perfect for a Jackie O-ish ensemble. A few pieces strike you as tasteful—an emerald brooch, a small sapphire and diamond pendant—but the larger pieces, which must have been handed down from older relatives, look as heavy and unattractive as Delia and Monty said they were. What's the point of holding on to them, that's what she said.

And then you hear something else. It isn't the author, but a different sound—from downstairs. A door. You freeze, kneeling on the bedroom floor before the jewelry box. Maybe it was your imagination, you tell yourself, knowing it was not. The scratching is getting louder now, and you strain to listen through it. Footsteps, downstairs. What are you going to tell her? You look down at the bright yellow gloves on your hands. Suddenly, the whole idea seems preposterous. Can we back up and erase this, you want to ask.

Carefully, you rise to your feet, and as you do, the wooden floor creaks.

"Hello?" calls a man's voice.

You say nothing, remain half-crouching, half-standing, for fear the floor will creak again. Could there be a real burglar? No, that would be even more preposterous.

"Delia, is that you?" The voice is followed by more footsteps from below.

Your heart is pounding now. This was not part of the plan. He's supposed to be out of the country. You hurriedly shove the jewelry box under the dresser, close the drawer, and slide into the master bathroom. Your only impulse is to hide. What else is there to do? The author's scratching grows louder, as do the slow footsteps from below.

"Delia, are you up there?"

A light from downstairs is flicked on and seeps into the bedroom, something drops to the floor with a thud, then, "I know *someone* is up there. I can hear you, you know."

After a moment, the footsteps move further away, then return.

"Hello?" the man calls from the bottom of the stairs. "Okay, let's cut the crap."

This is not what's supposed to happen. You look up at the ceiling as if you might catch the author's eye.

"I've got no patience for this. . . . I have a gun." The stairs begin to creak.

The man is not bluffing. You know that much. You saw the antique gun cases downstairs. You know he keeps a gun in the kitchen. Just waiting to use it, Graham once said. And now you're about to give him his opportunity. This cannot be happening. This *cannot* be happening. And yet the slow movement up the stairs continues. It occurs to you, as you crouch in front of the shower stall, that you really could be killed. This is Delia's novel. It could go on just fine without you. Maybe you were introduced to make yourself the victim of her father's bloodhunger. Maybe this book was never going to be about success or a love triangle or a stranger with a heart of gold. Maybe this is a family drama. About Delia, Graham, Mr. Benson. Maybe the author was following her father home this evening when you thought your break-in should have been observed. You're not writing this book. You have no way of knowing.

"Come on out, now."

The man must still be on the staircase. He's holding a pistol, no doubt. The one from the kitchen cabinet. You heard all about that, behind the bread box. And then your eyes rivet to the nightstand a few feet from the bathroom door. The kitchen cabinet and the nightstand—those are two places where Delia said he kept his guns. Without thinking, you yank the plastic glove off your right hand, steal out into the bedroom, and open the drawer of the nightstand. Inside is an unzipped leather pouch. You reach in and pull out a gun. You've never touched a gun before. It's heavier than you thought it would be.

Judging from the silence in the hallway, Mr. Benson has not moved, but he must have heard you open the drawer. You glance out the window beside the bathroom door. It drops onto a concrete patio. Even if you could make it out without getting shot, you'd probably hurt yourself in the fall and give Mr. Benson time to catch up. To shoot you, more likely. You can't die, you tell yourself. So what are you supposed to do? You dart back into the bathroom and drop to the floor, your back against the cabinets.

The pencil is scribbling more rapidly than you've ever heard before. You certainly have the author's attention. The stairs creak again, but the scratching of the pencil grows louder and louder, eclipsing the sound of the stairs, the pounding of your pulse. And when you see the man enter the bedroom, and when you see the flash of metal in his hand, and when you realize that the man has not spotted you yet, it all happens suddenly and without thought. In one brisk movement, you slide out of the bathroom, take aim, and fire the gun once at Mr. Benson's chest. The noise that comes out of him is something between a gasp and a cough. Then he falls backward, hitting the wall with a thud on the way down.

The red looks almost unnaturally bright. The white wall is spattered with blood, a puddle grows on the oak floor, and you have to turn away to keep your stomach from giving out. Your hand still shakes with the vibration of the gun. The gunshot echoes in your ears. It's all you can do to remain standing, so you step back into the bathroom and slide down to the floor, your back against the cabinets like before.

You just killed this man. This man who was about to kill you. And it was all so fast . . . so easy. You marvel that you didn't hesitate at the last minute, didn't seem to consider the possibility that you might be shot first, that you might miss, that the gun might have a safety or a lock of some sort, that the gun might not even be loaded. At the moment you felt compelled to shoot, you didn't question whether or not you would succeed.

Because the author *made* you shoot. That's what happened. *Of course* the gun was in easy reach. *Of course* it was loaded. *Of course* you hit the target in one shot. You came here to free Delia, and the author figured out a better way to do it. As a chill passes over you—the recognition that the man in the other room is dead because of you—you push the thought away. "It's just another character," you announce, your voice coming out louder than you intended. That was his role in the book. To get killed. A lot of books have characters who just walk in to get shot. Not a pretty role, but not a new one.

A click of the air conditioner startles you into action. You have to leave. Someone might have heard the gunshot, might have called the police. Without thinking, you become a character out of a million murder stories. You put your glove back on and use a washcloth to wipe off the gun. The scratching follows you back into the bedroom, where you try not to look at Mr. Benson's body as you return the gun to its leather pouch and run the washcloth over the handle of the nightstand drawer. You open a few dresser drawers and scatter the contents. Then you grab the jewelry box, along with a few credit cards you find on top of the dresser, and hurry over the body and out into the hallway.

The large suitcase at the foot of the stairs surprises you for a moment, but you don't allow yourself to be distracted. You move down the stairs and into the den, where you empty a desk drawer onto the floor and leave the computer and television askew as if someone attempted to carry them off. You sneak a glance outside, where there appears to be no SWAT team waiting for you. Then you grab a can of pinto beans from the kitchen pantry, return to the side door, and smash in a windowpane from the outside. Finally, you take a shopping bag from the pantry floor, throw in the jewelry box, credit cards, washcloth, and yellow gloves, and slip out of the house, leaving the door unlocked.

The Mercedes in the driveway frightens you for a moment, the engine still cooling down with a quiet ticking sound. You walk in measured steps to the sidewalk. You're terrified a neighbor might have heard the gunshot, might see you coming out of the house. But the houses are pretty far apart, and no one is out-side, and you feel some sense that the author will protect you. You turn left, walk slowly. Your car is parked around the corner. Two doors down, a teenage kid riding a bicycle darts out from beside a house. He cuts in front of you but doesn't look at you or your bag. The street is dark. Lights on in many windows.

Your car door slamming, the seatbelt clicking into place, the engine turning over—they sound conspicuously loud, even ac-companied by the roar of the author's pencil. Mr. Benson was just a character, you remind yourself. And *you* are just a charac-ter. Just doing what the author has you do. Why didn't you put something else in the bag to cover up the credit cards and the gloves? No matter. You're driving off and no one is noticing. You won't be caught. You can't be. Because this has become *your* book. *You* are the protagonist, not some yes-man, not some two-dimensional supporting character. Your escape is essential because this is the most exciting moment in the story so far. It's becoming the kind of book people can't put down, the kind they sell at the airport.

At home, no one sees you step out of your car, no one hears the jewelry box clank as you mount the stairs. You toss the gloves into the kitchen garbage can—they're dishwashing gloves, after all. Plus, there's no reason in the world why you would have robbed Mr. Benson, no possibility of anyone mak-ing the connection. You throw away the washcloth and penlight too, stash the jewelry box and credit cards in a suitcase beneath your bed. Only as you're brushing your teeth does it occur to you that you should have just put the jewelry box back in the dresser. Can't very well sell the pieces now—or show them to Delia.

But you'll figure that out later. For now, she'll have plenty of money and that's what matters. And as you lie down on the bed, your body suddenly overpowered by fatigue, you begin replaying the evening's adventure in your mind and try to imagine how you're being portrayed. The scratching, a comfort, remains with you; slowly, it lulls you to sleep.

THE MORNING AFTER you kill someone is a strange time. You pull a bagel out of the toaster. It's an Asiago bagel, and it tastes good by itself, but you add a thin layer of garlic and herb cream cheese anyway. You eat it. It's good. Only now do you recall that you forgot to eat dinner last night. So you were hungry. Are hungry. The television has nothing to report. You glance out the window beside the table. Do you expect to see FBI agents? Detectives? Demons? You prefer not to think about it. You dress, pulling out whatever you find closest to the center of the closet. It hardly matters; most things look the same. The author is with you, of course. You have to take off your shirt just as soon as you put it on because you forgot to shave. You wonder if you'll cut yourself. You don't. Nothing happens.

You brush your hair, and in the mirror, you notice a spot of coffee on your shirt. The shirt is navy, so it's barely visible. Maybe you can dab it with a washcloth. Except that . . . no, you weren't wearing this shirt when you had breakfast. This isn't even the shirt you picked out for today. This is yesterday's shirt. It's not coffee. It's blood.

Your mind could take either of two diverging paths, and you opt for the latter. It's just a stain. Probably will come out. Normally you have your clothes laundered, but this seems like an occasion for you to wait out the spin cycle at the Laundromat yourself. You'll do a load of darks tonight. You pick up yesterday's khaki pants from the floor. They look fine. But you can do lights too, while you're at it.

You go to work, and throughout the day the scratching seems to come and go, but you don't listen very carefully. There's nothing about Mr. Benson on the local websites, but that's not how you really expect to hear the news. So you and the author both wait, mark the time. The hours pass, but slowly. You're supposed to be pulling together market data on other Italian corporations that have successfully penetrated the U.S. market. Pasta and olive oil manufacturers hardly seem comparable to a bank, but your job is to put the material into animated slide presentations and pretend it's significant. You keep losing your place in the articles you're reading, and you try not to think about what jail is like. Even though Mr. Benson was just a character—and you are, too—you live in a world where people don't think that way. Your world has jail. There are a lot of bad people in jail.

Could this turn into a book about jail?

No, there's been too much emphasis on life outside of jail for this to turn into one of those stories. The author has invested too much time in you—and in Delia and what you're doing to help her. Everything is set up so nicely. And who in the world would connect you to the shooting? Still, you might want to be careful when you take out the trash tonight. There might be blood on the gloves.

The afternoon passes, as it was bound to, and the hour at the Laundromat around the corner from your apartment. Then eight o'clock approaches and arrives and you're walking up to Lilly's. And it feels as if you've just arrived in this body. You feel so conscious of your legs, the sensation of your feet making contact with the concrete outside the bar and then the wooden floor inside, where Delia smiles and raises her eyebrows and offers you a big wave. There are only four other people in the bar besides her. It's a Tuesday. Martini night. She's sipping a pink martini.

"Hello, dearest Daniel," she says. There is a glimmer in her eyes, like the glimmer you see in a character's eyes in a movie. Like the kind of glimmer the photographer inserts so the audience says, "Oh, look at the glimmer in her eyes." That's what it looks like to you. She has no idea. She has her father's eyes.

"Graham is in the john," she tells you. "Listen, I didn't tell him I went to your apartment Saturday night. He might have been upset, because . . ." She lets you fill in the blank, but it seems more in the interest of time than decorum. "But everything's worked out now," she says, hurrying on. "Thanks for humoring me the other night. It was nice to just be as melodramatic as I felt."

"Oh, that's fine," you say. "Glad to help."

Glad to help?

"Did you get my message?" she asks.

"Message?" you say. What in the world could she be talking about? But—oh, yes, right. "No," you say. "My phone has been doing strange things. I'm sorry."

"It's no big deal. I just was asking if I happened to leave a set of keys anywhere. I can't find them, and I wondered if they fell out of my purse at your place."

"Gosh, I'm sorry. Were you locked out?" you ask. Good. Good thinking.

"Oh, no," she says. "They were just an extra set."

"Well, I didn't see them, but I'll definitely check when I get home."

Graham walks up and slaps your shoulder, and when he heads over to the bar, Delia puts a finger to her lips to mime "shhh." The gesture drips of bad writing, and you almost roll your eyes. But you don't. Instead, you say hello to Graham, who returns with a fresh martini for himself and one for you. He talks about dog-walking and how people treat their pets so much better than their children. Then Jon arrives, and Monty, and Delia invites everyone to a Fourth of July barbecue on Friday, and you wonder if that will end up happening—seems unlikely. The invitation reminds Jon of a past barbecue that involved an electrician and a salad bar and *Sunset Boulevard*, and you try to listen and laugh in the right places, but you aren't paying enough attention to catch the gist of it. Because you're too distracted. By Delia's face.

It's creepy, the resemblance. Mostly the eyes and the sharp, angular nose. The brow is sort of similar. Unless you're misremembering. You don't recall taking a careful look at Mr. Benson. Maybe this is a fake memory that the author wants to insert for effect. You scan your memory of last night: ballerina figurines on a white bookshelf, a childhood picture of Delia, gray cabinets in the bathroom—that was real, right? And the resemblance, it feels pretty real too, even if you didn't think about it then. Her eyes are distinct, unusually dark. You remember noticing them on the night you met her, admiring her eyes from across the booth—the same booth, in fact, where you're all sitting now.

"So I said, take it all," Jon says, and Delia, Graham, and Monty burst into laughter. You try to force a laugh, but it sounds wholly unnatural, so you fake a cough instead.

"Are you okay?" Delia asks.

"Just swallowed wrong," you say.

Such light spirits at the table. Well, to all of them, it's a fairly normal night. Except for the fact that Delia spent the night at your house over the weekend. But who knows that? Monty, maybe? Probably not. Graham seems like his usual self. He probably has no idea that you even heard about their fight. Or his source of employment. The author is scratching away above you—or *around* or *beside* or *in*—and you wonder if you're missing something in the conversation that the author might be recording. But what could it possibly be? No, you and the author just need to sit through this and see if anything is going to happen. There's no other way to find out. Unless—

Chekhov.

"What?" Delia says.

To you. Now everyone's looking at you. "Nothing," you say.

Jon laughs. "You just shouted 'Chekhov.'"

Okay, well that's embarrassing. "I just thought of something," you tell them, "that, you know, reminded me of Chekhov. Sorry." Smooth. Very smooth.

You slip out from the booth to go to the men's room, and Graham is laughing as you go. "That is so random," he says.

No. Nothing is random. If a gun shows up in the first act, it has to go off by the end of the story. Something like that. It was in the Corrone book. As soon as Delia mentioned the gun to you, it had to go off somewhere in the book. Planting the seeds, watering the garden. You're so dense. The author isn't waiting it out, isn't watching and recording. You didn't just *become* the protagonist. This whole thing has been planned. Corrone has two, three chapters on outlines and plotting. A book can't be written off the cuff. Look at how hard it was when you tried to write just a little story. Everything that's happened so far was planned out from the beginning: the shooting, the stupid letters you wrote for Graham, the night you hooked up with Delia—and further back—the night you were mugged, even the day you were born. It's all been building. And what you're in now is kind of a modern-day fairy tale: hero slays the dragon to free the girl. And since you're the hero, you're going to get the girl in the end. Because that's what always happens in these kinds of stories.

It's incredible that you didn't realize this earlier. You take a couple of deep breaths and wash your face. The scratching is still with you. This chapter isn't over yet. You need to go back out there, but your heart is pounding and your face is red. You need to calm down. Focus—or stop focusing. This should be a normal night. It is. No one knows anything yet. It's just a Tuesday.

"So, Chekhov," Graham says when you slide back into the booth, "how's the book coming along?"

"Oh," you say, "it's, um, coming."

"Slow going?" Graham asks.

"No, the . . . ah . . . the plot has actually thickened, as the saying goes. I think it's going pretty well."

"That's great," Delia says, raising her pink glass to you in a familiar silent toast. "Look forward to reading it—when you're ready."

You hope she'll be happy—relieved, at least. Eventually. She'll be sad at first. So much has to happen before the happy part, and you dread the wait. The body hasn't even been found. Or maybe it has. No, the police would tell Delia pretty quickly. It must smell awful by now. For a moment, the image of the blood on the wall pops into your mind. Then the scene backs up, and you're standing in the bedroom, the hunted, heart pounding. You grab the gun and fire. He could have shot back at any moment. But you made an amazing shot.

"Martini, anyone?" Monty asks, balancing three glasses in his hands.

"Definitely," you say, pushing your empty glass aside.

Delia reaches across the table and rests a hand on yours. "You're getting a little drunk, Mr. Fischer." Your first encounter rushes back to you again. The seduction. The shedding of clothes. Her little grunts on the sofa, that final, satisfied sigh. Her hand feels warm, moist. And she pulls back only after a long moment, after you register her naughty grin. There is something naughty about it, isn't there? That has got to be a sign. What's the word? Foreshadowing. It's all going to happen again.

STILL NO NEWS the next morning, and you have to get the keys out of your apartment, so you call Delia to see if she's free for breakfast. But she's on the train, and her cell connection is horrible, and she tells you to just bring them to the barbecue on Friday, and that's when you get cut off. Of course, anything could happen in the next few days, in the next few hours even. How unobservant can the neighbors be? So you pick up a croissant and a vanilla latte to go and drive directly to her office with the keys. She's surprised to see you, but grateful. "You really didn't have to," she says.

You decide to be the confident man courting. That's where this is going, anyway. "I wanted to buy you breakfast," you tell her with the nonchalant smile you practiced in the car. It works. She gives you a long hug, then sends you out the door.

It's Monty who comes to deliver the news the next morning.

You've already played out every imaginable scenario in your mind—a call to Delia from the police during your quick visit to her office, Jon's somber face meeting you on an appointed night out, Delia's hysterical voice on the telephone, an ambiguous but foreboding item on the evening news, a plainclothes detective striding into Lilly's, a police car pulling up at Delia and Graham's barbecue. Hearing your name called from the office doorway, raising your eyes to see the sharply dressed figure in the threshold, you're certain of what Monty is there to say, and you flip through your mental screening room to another scene you have already envisioned.

In spite of your social outings over the past couple of months, you and Monty have not developed a parallel camaraderie during the business day. His office is four floors above yours, you use different conference rooms and coffee pots, and you attend few of the same meetings. The few times you've run into him at the office, he's greeted you with only a curt acknowledgment of your name, the preceding "hello" or "good morning" implied. So Monty's solicitous tone today and his very presence in the doorway can have only one explanation.

"Have you heard?" Monty asks, as you knew he would.

You bring out your curious face. "Heard what?"

"About Delia's father."

Raise your eyebrows. "Her father?"

"He's been killed."

The wind is knocked out of you. You've been holding your breath to facilitate this reaction, and you carry it off with some degree of success. Delia just found out herself this morning, Monty explains. A delivery man saw a window broken by the side door of her father's house and called the police. They came, searched the house, and found Mr. Benson dead in his bedroom. It appears he was killed trying to interfere with a robbery. Delia didn't even know her father was back in town.

"Oh my God," you say at intervals. "Poor Delia. How horrible."

"I'm heading off to the police station now."

"Should I come?" you ask, rising.

"No," Monty says. "Graham may have taken Delia home already. They need someone to identify the body and . . . well, she's not exactly up to it."

"Wow," you say, and a chill envelops you. The image of a corpse in one of those morgue drawers they have on television draws attention to the reality of the situation. But that's where corpses are put, you tell yourself. That's the aftermath of a shooting.

"The funeral will probably be this weekend," Monty adds. A long pause follows, and you notice that Monty has barely stepped inside your small office. In the version you imagined, Monty closed the door and sat in the guest chair, sometimes covered his face with his hands. But in fact, Monty is deadly calm. Rigid, but calm. "Anyway," he continues, shifting his weight back toward the hallway, "I should head out. I just thought you'd want to know. It'll be all over the news soon."

Throughout the day, you check the Internet for reports on the murder. During your lunch hour, you sit at a hole-in-the-wall deli where you know the television will be on, but you can't manage to eat your club sandwich and find it difficult even to sit still. Not until two o'clock, an hour after lunch, does the first story show up on a local website. Its appearance is such a relief to you, and after reading it the first time, you pull out the sandwich you could not abide earlier. The report details an overnight burglary that ended in a shoot-out. The inaccuracy of the story is distancing yet familiar, like watching a movie or reading a book. You picture yourself in the burglar's position as if the fiction were true. It is midnight, and you are robbing the house, clad in black, truck parked in the driveway. The door opens, a shot is fired, then another and another. You run upstairs, pull a gun out of your back pocket, and fire as the rifle-toting homeowner walks into the room.

The television report at six tells a more accurate story. No reference to a shoot-out, though the homeowner was carrying a gun. The murder weapon belonged to the deceased. The burglar made off with some valuables but clearly left before he could finish the job. Interviews with neighbors, who have nothing interesting to say. Then on to news of the latest highway construction debacle. You flip channels, watch the report on a second station, watch reports again at seven and eleven, and go to bed with little concern. The truth is out. The man was shot by a burglar. Police never find burglars. No one on earth would suspect you because you have no reason to have gone there. The end.

In bed that night, you wonder if those girls who mugged you were ever caught. Probably not. That wouldn't be a very good ending. Maybe they went on to college, law school. Or maybe one made good and the other didn't. They could have gotten involved in some more sophisticated crime—become con artists or art thieves or something. Could be the start of a fun serial. Do they ever think about you, you wonder. Wouldn't they be surprised if they could see you now?

Graham

GRAHAM PAUSES OUTSIDE the apartment door. He hears it. He was hoping she'd still be out with Monty or in Winchester with her family, but she's back, sitting on the sofa where he left her five hours ago, staring at the television, flanked by the cat on one side and a mug of coffee or tea or wine on the other. He'll have to stop on the way across the room, maybe sit down beside her—no across from her—and ask her how everything went. Please, Lord, don't let her cry. Not right yet. Ten minutes. That's all he needs.

Graham pushes his hair behind his ear without thinking, then grunts and wipes his hand vigorously on his jeans. Okay, let's do it, he tells himself, then takes a deep breath and unlocks the door. Delia slouches in a pink bathrobe under a mountain of quilts on the sofa. Her dark hair is matted, her face white. The lights are off; only the television set glows.

"Hi," she says without redirecting her eyes.

"Hey," he says.

"Everything okay? You were gone for a while."

"Yeah," he says, hesitating before seating himself on the loveseat catty-corner from her. "Just had to stop by a few houses. Walk two dogs."

"Mmm," she says, now turning to face him.

Graham feels caked in the stench. He hates touching the furniture. He hated even touching the doorknob. He can't bring himself to pet Myra, who lies between them on the coffee table. He wishes Delia would turn back to the television, wishes she had fallen asleep.

"Did everything go okay?" he asks. "With the funeral home and stuff?"

"All set," she says quietly.

"And your family got in all right?"

"Everyone's here," she tells him. "They're at my aunt's house."

"Good," he says. But he doesn't know what to say next. This morning, he offered to help pick people up at the airport and go to the funeral home with her. When she said not to worry about it, that Monty would go with her and her aunt, Graham didn't know whether to feel relieved or offended. It's not like he wanted to go.

"Are you all right?" Delia asks with a little more life to her voice than he's heard in the past three days.

"Yeah," he says, rising. "It's just been a long night. I need to take a shower. One of those dogs kept licking me." The words taste vile, and he heads for the bathroom.

He stashes the wad of bills inside his shaving kit, then piles the clothes on the floor, making a mental note to do laundry as soon as possible. He turns on the shower, and as always, the water takes some time to warm up, but today it doesn't seem to get hot enough. He needs it to be hot. Very hot.

The evening did not go well at all. He had a funny feeling when he spotted the guy—fifties, short, with a shiny bald head and a big belly, wire-rim glasses and thick pale hands and forearms covered in black hair. Graham was tempted to leave, but the Silent Owl was almost empty, and the man spotted him right away and offered a grin that was at once disarming and unsettling. And Graham needed the cash.

So talkative. The man chatted during an interminable train ride to his apartment. Followed by a long walk. Graham nodded, looked straight forward. Talk of weather, the man's Pekingese, and compliments. Lots of hungry compliments. Then inside, after greeting the Pekingese, the man stripped down to a black bikini, his pale flesh leaping out on all sides, and still the talking continued. Graham was so tall, so sexy, so strong.

The cramped apartment smelled like dirty clothes and dirty Pekingese. The sheets on the unmade bed looked gray. Discarded clothes cluttered the floor. The man had a powerful, unpleasant odor: sweat and desire. And he kept talking. "Call me your pig boy," he said. Pig boy! God, of all things. Not only did it sound childish and tawdry, but *pig boy*—just what the kids called Graham at school, though for very different reasons. Growing up on a hog farm, which infects the air for miles in all directions, a kid learns to expect the taunts. Graham's brothers reveled in the title. The Pig Brothers, they were. Graham was not proud of the distinction.

"Come on! Just say it! I'm your pig boy, right?" The man was lying on his back now, bikini shed.

"Boy, you need to shut up," Graham said in his best Texas accent.

But the man didn't obey. He laughed. He said, "*Oink, oink.*"

So Graham ignored him, slipped on a condom, and stared at the stain on the paper window shade across from him. He tried thinking about other things—about girls from magazine pictures and from movies, about people who have to work all week—but these thoughts did little *oink* to transport him. He took a mental inventory *oink* of men who'd paid him so far and tried to decide which ones were most obedient, most *oink* agreeable. He tried not to imagine *oink* the scent of this man infecting his body, but it was difficult *oink* to ignore, and Graham was fading with each squeal from beneath him, and finally—"Call me your pig boy!" "Faggot, shut up!"—Graham reached out and slapped the man, backhanded, across the face.

For an instant, the man was silent. His mouth was opened in surprise, his fleshy cheek red where Graham had hit him. Graham took a step back. He wondered if he should apologize, if he would still be paid, if he should run. And that's when the hot wetness shot him on the cheek. It sprayed across the sheets. It landed on Graham's shirt, which was hanging from the headboard. It went everywhere. And before Graham could make it to the bathroom, he felt a drop run down his chin and drip to his chest.

"Oh yeah," the man squeaked.

Graham hesitated at the sight of the moist, wrinkled bath towel, then went ahead and used it to wipe off his face, chest, and shirt. The scent of mildew and wetness mingled with the ammonia, and just as he was wondering if this could possibly be his life, Graham saw the man behind him in the mirror and remembered. The guy worked at the New England Conservatory. He taught voice, mostly tenors. Never trained

Delia, as far as Graham knew, and Graham certainly never studied with him, but he had seen those hungry eyes before in the halls, in the cafeteria.

He had to wait in the living room for the money. The man went to the bathroom and washed the sweat off his face and talked to his Pekingese and told Graham how hot he was, and only after what felt like hours did the man return and fish into his pants pocket for a series of wrinkled twenties and tens. The counting process was slow, but Graham was not in a position to complain. He thought about HIV and crabs and all the other diseases the man might have. The word *fungus* jumped into Graham's mind. This is someone who'd have fungus problems.

Finally, the man offered the stack of bills to Graham. "It's not quite two hundred dollars," he said, "but I'm not sure you really put on a two-hundred-dollar show, you know?"

Graham couldn't look at him. He almost didn't want to accept the bills, damp with what he hoped was just sweat, but he needed them. So he took the money and shoved it in his pocket and headed for the door as quickly as he could without running. And he pretended not to hear the man's question about setting up another meeting.

Even the second rinse doesn't seem to get the night out of his hair, and Graham lathers in another mound of shampoo. He hurriedly crushes a washcloth over every inch of flesh again. Soon the tepid water will run out and the nozzle will rain ice. And soon he will have to return to Delia. She'll be sitting in the same place, a flicker of curiosity in her otherwise vacant eyes.

After toweling himself dry, Graham pulls on a pair of boxers and ventures a few steps into the living room. "Are you coming to bed?" he asks.

"In a little bit," she says without turning her head.

He wants to hold her, to wrap himself around her, to show her how much he loves her. He wants to be inside of her, and he wants her to want him, too. But it's too soon. She needs time. He should really go to a doctor, get himself checked. But then they'll be good again.

Graham starts to turn into the bedroom, then paces back to stand beside the television. "Do you want to drive out to the beach or something after all this? Just get out of town, get away from everything?"

Delia shrugs and turns toward him. "Maybe," she says, her gaze falling just below his eyes. "We'll see. I just want to get through tomorrow."

"Okay," he says, retreating slowly into the bedroom. The breeze created by his stride chills his chest. It's going to be difficult to get to sleep.

Daniel

THE RED BRICK church in Winchester looks vaguely like the one your parents used to drag you to every Easter and Christmas and on the odd pre- or post-gambling Sunday. The building is at least two hundred years old, as are the pew cushions, if comfort level is any indication. You heard the author's scratching a minute ago, but now it's hard to make out over the sound of the rain beating against the stained-glass windows. The pencil is probably still scribbling away somewhere nearby, though it strikes you as a bit distasteful that the author has decided to write this scene.

There must be more than seventy mourners shuffling in and out of the pews. Almost everyone wears black in expensive-looking fabrics and designs. Scores of broad-shouldered men with gray hair, women trying to look fifty, and well-manicured young couples. Delia sits crumpled in the second row beside

Graham and a lot of people you've never seen before. She saw you arrive, but she hasn't turned around since. She just keeps looking straight ahead or down. Monty is walking up and down the aisle looking officious. You haven't seen Jon.

Of course, no one wants to go to a funeral. No one wants to go to church. You used to give your parents a hard time about it—yours was hardly a religious household—but they liked to say it was either Jesus or a lucky star that was watching over your family, and since things always seemed to work out in the end, they couldn't risk letting go of either one. You started staying home on principle, though holiday services do tend to have good music. Here there's no choir, and the organ music is so "soothing" that you can feel the quotation marks. Why is the author interested in this? Isn't a funeral the kind of run-of-the-mill ritual that has to happen but that everyone would gladly skip over? A roadblock to the next chapter of life. You have to sit through it, and Graham and Monty, but why should the readers be subjected to the dreariness? "Jump ahead five pages," you want to whisper. You mouth the words.

At length, the service begins with all the bells, whistles, and efficiency of Catholicism. A little Latin, rising, kneeling, sitting, and twenty minutes later, one of Mr. Benson's college buddies is standing before the room talking about what a funny and charitable person he was: whoopee cushion pranks in college, chamber of commerce and United Way, scholarship fund at his alma mater, great husband, great father. You can distinguish Delia's sobs from twenty rows back, or you think you can. There is a lot of sniffling in the room. Many Kleenex sought from purses. Only one other person sits in the pew beside you, a man Mr. Benson's age in full Navy garb. His lip appears to tremble, but it may be the dim light.

After the first eulogy, a clean-cut young man in a black suit steps up to the pulpit and, with admirable composure, starts talking about his father. His *father?* When *we* were kids, he says. So Delia has a brother. Younger. Maybe twenty years old. She never mentioned him before, which seems odd. But he talks about family trips to London and Brussels, Christmases together. He says he doesn't consider himself unlucky to have lost both his parents but lucky to have had them. Your eyes start to tear up, and you hear yourself sniffle a couple of times. It's a touching scene, really. A bit sentimental, perhaps, but still . . . You want to shake the kid's hand. You want to apologize. But no, it wasn't your idea. And besides, this good husband and father would have shot you on sight if you'd given him the chance. Then this would be your funeral.

No, yours would not be so well attended.

The rain stops in time for the burial service, which is brief—far shorter than the drive from the church or to the aunt's house. You drive alone and have to park two blocks away. The house is a big colonial affair with two sitting rooms off the entrance hall furnished with ancient sofas and hard-backed chairs that look about as comfortable as the church pews. It's not until you get to the front of the long receiving line that you realize you're wearing the same shoes you had on when you killed him.

"I'm sorry," you say to the brother, who gives you a firm handshake. You can't say anything to Delia. She looks so lost. You hug her, and she whispers, "Thank you for coming," as she said to the woman before you and says again to the person behind you. You shuffle on through a crowd of sympathetic murmuring. "So terrible." "Tragic." "Too young."

"Spitting image," says a familiar voice a few minutes later. It's Jon, who has sidled up to you in one of the sitting rooms. You realize you've been staring at the receiving line, at the brother, in fact. And yes, now that Jon mentions it, the dark eyes are the same, the nose, the coloring, the height. "Charlie's like the frat-boy version of her," Jon adds, "only with natural hair."

"Delia dyes her hair?" you ask.

Jon rolls his eyes. "I hope you're kidding me. Nature does not make that shade of black."

Charlie's hair is a rich chocolate brown, and you try to transfer the color to Delia's curls, but without much success. "He was very eloquent at the funeral," you say. "Did you hear?"

"No, I can't go to funerals. Makes me crazy and doesn't do anyone any good. Not like I have the power to raise the dead."

"I didn't know Delia had a brother," you say just as Monty walks up. "Do they get along?"

"Oh, sure," Monty says. "He's at Stanford now, but he used to come to her concerts when he was in high school. They talk on the phone every week or so."

Standing between Jon and Monty, you realize that Charlie is like a cross between the two: He has Jon's universally good looks and confident air, but exudes money and breeding the way Monty likes to and Delia doesn't.

The silence grows as the three of you watch the receiving line, which has no end in sight. "So how is she holding up?" Jon asks after a spell. "I haven't really talked to her."

"Hard to say," Monty says with a shrug. "Crazy to lose both parents so young—and to have him murdered like that, in the house where she grew up. It's a lot to take."

Not your fault, you remind yourself. Not your plan. "Do the police have any leads?" you ask.

"Not that I've heard," Monty says, "but all I know is what they say on the news."

Again the three of you watch the receiving line, and eventually Jon slips off, then Monty. You stay only a bit longer, overhearing bits of conversation about how sad it all is, how brave the kids are, how wealthy they'll be soon.

And it's odd to be the agent of responsibility, standing alone and unnoticed in the back of the room, observing the consequences while sipping the family's wine and eating their cubed cheese off family china that Mr. Benson must have used. You permit yourself to wonder once again if there's any way the police might think to connect you to the shooting. But no, only someone reading this book could possibly see a connection. You're Delia's friend. You have a job. There are plenty of criminals in Boston.

You feel an inexplicable thrill pass through you. "What are you saying right now?" you'd like to ask the author. The sorrow in the room is picturesque. Delia's sadness, more profound than you anticipated it would be, is temporary like all strong emotion. There could be some aesthetic value in all this, depending on how the scene is written. Maybe that's what the author wants the reader to see.

Jon

"THE POLICE STOPPED by to talk to me again today," Graham says as soon as Jon can maneuver his way to the back of the Silent Owl. "This is the third time."

Jon knew this wasn't going to be a fun visit, but a friendly hello or thanks-for-coming would have been all right. Graham looks like shit—he has huge bags under his eyes, his overshirt looks like it's been balled up for a decade, the hair could really stand a trim, and he's ashed all over his sneakers. Jon settles into a half-stuffed easy chair artlessly repaired with electrical tape, then asks the passing waitress for a cup of coffee, before responding. "Are they accusing you of anything?" he asks quietly.

"No. But I think they'd like to figure out a way to make it my fault."

Not surprising. But Jon just nods. He can wait. Let Graham bring it up.

"I can't tell if they know about . . . you know."

Here it comes. Jon studies the floor. "What do you tell them?" he asks.

"As little as possible," Graham snickers.

"And what do you tell Delia?"

Graham drops his eyes.

So much for patience. "Fuck it," Jon mumbles. "I saw your ad reappear. The week of the damned funeral. Does Delia know?"

Graham sucks down the last of his cigarette, then crushes the butt in the ashtray. "It's temporary."

"Shall I take that as a 'no'?"

The waitress interrupts them with Jon's coffee, and Graham pulls another cigarette from his breast pocket and burns through two matches before he can get it lit.

"God," Jon says, trying to force his rage into a whisper. "Are you so anxious to give her a venereal disease? Do you long for herpes? I'd threaten to tell her myself, but in case you hadn't noticed, her father was just shot to death, and I'm not evil."

"Look, I want to stop."

"Then stop."

"I can't."

"Because . . . ?"

Graham sighs and tosses down the rest of his Bloody Mary. "We're kind of broke," he says. "I know she'll eventually inherit something, but right now—I mean, I haven't worked much, and now she's stopped going to the office. Hell, I'd be glad for her to give up that job. I just keep telling myself I need to stomach this to cover the bills until the money comes in. Does that make sense?"

"Barely," Jon says. Graham's breath is toxic, between the smoke and the vodka. It's a wonder anyone pays him. "There are other jobs, you know," Jon adds.

"I know."

"And can you really blame the police for investigating the lying hustler boyfriend who has no money? It's not such a crazy mental leap."

"Jesus, I didn't—"

"Of course, you didn't. I'm just saying, if the police have taken an interest in you, maybe it's the universe's way of pointing you in another direction."

Graham coughs into his hand. "Maybe so. But I think I'm going to cut back to just a few regulars I can trust, so if I stop now or in a month or two, it really won't make much difference."

Jon checks his watch. In half an hour, he'll meet up with Mark for dinner. What a relief that'll be. Three dinner dates in three weeks—it's like a record. Practically marriage.

After a minute, Jon asks, "How is Delia?"

"Peachy," Graham replies. "She's having dinner with Daniel tonight. Isn't that interesting?"

He is such a child. Sometimes Jon feels his age around Graham.

"I'm sure he has a thing for her," Graham continues. "Don't you think?"

Jon measures his words. Of course it has crossed his mind. He knows she spent the night at Daniel's house recently; she asked Jon to cover for her. But she insisted that nothing happened, and Jon's inclined to believe her. In any event, one thing's for sure: that Daniel is a helper. Jon half expects him to launch a secret investigation and track down the murderer himself. He can just picture Daniel smiling awkwardly as he presents the criminal, bound and gagged. Calmly, Jon says, "He knows you two are together."

"Yeah, but I don't trust him," Graham says. "Do you?"

"I'm sorry, your halo distracted me. Did we forget what you're doing?"

"Would you just answer the question?"

Jon checks his watch again. It's time to go. "Under the circumstances," he says, "it's difficult to fault Daniel for having dinner with her."

Delia

GIORGIO'S FINGERS ARE crushing the small of her back, and it feels so good she almost feels guilty. Should she be allowed to experience such pleasure after what's happened? Delia usually gets a forty-minute massage, but today she paid for a full ninety minutes. He took his time untying her neck and shoulders, and now he's inching his way down her back.

The funeral is finally over. And the burial. The family has dispersed. Charlie offered to stay and help, but she insisted that he go back to California. He's in the middle of a summer internship, and then his semester will start and there will be soccer practice for him to throw himself into. He's not much older than she was when their mother died. If ever there was a time to play the good big sister . . .

So she said she'd take care of it—the lawyers, the house,

the police. The first wave of activity seems to have passed, though some detective interviewed Graham again this morning. Such a waste of time. If it wasn't a burglar, it was probably some sweatshop slave or former employee her dad screwed over. There are bound to be plenty of candidates. Of course, no one wants to hear that.

What everyone wants to hear is how she's doing and what she's up to. With the women at work, it's like a competition to send the sympathy card with the biggest flowers etched on the cover or with the most dramatic calligraphy inside. We feel your pain, they say. We would do anything for you—and they underline *anything*. We're familiar with sympathy at the McKlein Lupus Foundation. Just try us. We've been sympathizing for years. Call us *anytime*.

With the out-of-town relatives and family friends and people from high school, it's what-are-you-up-to. What are you up to these days? Do you have any big shows coming up? Did you have to cancel any performances for the funeral? Of course, Delia didn't even have a date at the Methodist Home to cancel. More than once, she was tempted to just acknowledge that she's been throwing her youth away. But no one wants to hear that either.

Giorgio pushes the sheet aside and moves his hands further down. He'll work the muscles in her right leg first, finding places she didn't even know were tense and kneading the pain away. His hands are always firm but gentle, and he smells like eucalyptus, and the release he gives her is almost arousing at times. Or maybe it is arousing. When Delia first discovered Giorgio years ago, she and Jon used to joke that a good massage was a sanctioned act of infidelity. Of course, Graham made that joke a lot less funny.

A wave of tension passes through her body, but Giorgio

must be able to feel it, because his movements intensify. Delia kept Graham at arm's length for much of the funeral weekend, and in a way she feels bad; but he doesn't fit in well with her family, and besides, he's so unpredictable. She can always count on Monty to take care of whatever needs to be taken care of. Graham isn't like that. Graham is . . . well, it's hard to say what he's like these days.

Giorgio moves to her left leg now, and his hands tell her she should give in. When Delia first arrived at the spa, he gave her a knowing hug but spared her the sympathetic words. He has other ways of helping her feel better, and that's why she's here. She should let him take care of her. She will let him. She'll give herself up to the experience. The scent of eucalyptus and the sound of running water and the feeling of his fingers on her body slowly merge. There is a rhythm to the movements and the sound and to the heaviness of her body, and she is both asleep and awake, and soon there is nothing but the rushing waters and his eucalyptus hands pressing against her.

When the sound of water stops, signaling the end of her session, she returns to herself. It takes a moment. She blushes when she looks up. Giorgio is stepping out of the room to let her dress, but before he leaves, she catches his eye and he flashes her one of his reassuring smiles. He's Italian, with dark brown hair and olive skin. Average height, much smaller than Graham, with a build that's compact but sinewy, like Daniel's. He's a nice-looking guy, but he always looks especially handsome to her after a massage. Today is no exception.

Harvard Square is bright and loud after the calm of the spa, and it's such a disappointment to have to return to reality. Slowly, Delia moves her body toward the T station and down the escalator. The train meets her almost instantly, and it rushes her back toward her apartment and her life. The mail will have come. There will be cards and letters. It's hard to imagine writing the thank-you notes she's going to have to write—for the flowers, for the kind note, for the gift made in honor of her dead father. How is she going to write those words? How is she going to go back to the office and face those curious, sympathetic faces? How can she set foot in that house again? *If you believe you can do something, then you can do it*, her mother used to say. And that actually worked for math tests and play auditions in high school, but does it apply to grown-up things, too?

Well, today she doesn't have to make any decisions. She'll glance at the mail and turn on the television, and then it will get dark, and then she'll go see Daniel. She surprised herself, actually, agreeing to meet him for dinner. Most phone calls she hasn't returned; most invitations sound unappealing. But he's easy to be around, to talk to. In spite of all that's happened, there's no underlying sense of judgment with him. It's refreshing.

Davis Square is only two stops away, and when Delia steps out into the station, there is Broadway Lady waiting for her. Most people are at work—it's a little after three—so she's singing to an empty house. Just a few students and retirees pass through, a young mother and her children, and Delia. She stops to listen. "I get ill . . ." Broadway Lady sings in her loud soprano voice. The words that follow are incomprehensible. Then there's *paws* and *silky*. "Would you PULL . . ." she shrieks.

She's singing "Look at Me, I'm Sandra Dee" from *Grease*. What does that mean?
Why does it have to mean anything?

Delia digs through her purse and finds one dollar bill and then another. Slowly she approaches Broadway Lady, who is standing on a bench against the back wall. In front of her is a cardboard box with a handful of coins in it. And who is this woman underneath all that pink hair? Up close, she's not a million years old, as Delia and Graham always assumed she must be. She looks weathered, certainly, but she's probably in her forties or fifties. The woman smiles when Delia drops the bills in the box, but she doesn't stop singing. Nor does she stop when Delia walks up the stairs, leaving the station temporarily empty.

Doesn't every little girl believe she can grow up to be a star, Delia thinks. A singer or an actress or a ballerina. Outside the station, Delia turns left and crosses the street. Maybe she'd be better off if she hadn't gotten her hopes up so many times. What if that's the real problem? Maybe she's only two or three decades away from putting on a wig and singing in subway stations herself. For the amusement of pretentious wannabe kids who will go on to do nothing more impressive with their own lives.

Daniel

THE THING IS to make her see the bright side of it all.

No, the thing is to make her see this as an opportunity. Or maybe to see you as an opportunity. Or everything.

Damn, it's difficult to think. You're not getting enough sleep. Are you eating well? It's hard to remember.

You're meeting Delia for dinner at a new Chinese-Indian fusion restaurant in Central Square, but now you're late because you can't find a parking place. It's like every person in the city has decided to descend upon Central Square at once. So you're driving in ever-widening circles, and twice already a car has pulled out of a space behind you after it was too late for you to back up and get it. She's probably there already. Maybe she left.

"I need a goddamned parking place!" you announce.

The scratching just began at some point. Now if you were

writing this book, you would make a parking place materialize right about now, because how much time should be wasted circling? The reader is waiting for you to arrive at the restaurant, and with every passing minute, you're getting later for what could be a momentous encounter.

She agreed to dinner. Shouldn't you be *less* nervous now? But it doesn't really matter, does it? Because no matter what you should feel, your heart is thumping, and your neck aches with tension. How will the conversation go? Does she have feelings for you? She has to have feelings for you. Maybe she'll suggest running away together. You could leave tonight. But you have no money. Not much, anyway. You could hock a piece of jewelry.

Okay, how stupid are you?

"Could we have a parking place, please?" you shout.

The car in front of you is inching along slower than death. You can't even see a person in the driver's seat. Does the author sometimes forget to put people places where they should be? That would be funny. Not laugh-out-loud funny, but kind of funny. You pound on the horn. A finger rises from behind the driver's seat of the car to flip you off. Maybe it's a toddler. You turn at the next corner.

With or without any authorial aid—and you're inclined to think *without*—you find a spot off Mass. Ave. about eight blocks from the restaurant. You can walk quickly. Or maybe you should run. You can run fast. No, you might sweat. You're sweating a little already. And if she saw you outside, running, that would be pathetic.

It's Friday night, and as you hurry down the street, well-dressed young couples seem to be meandering in and out of every doorway. Your black pants and blue cotton sweater strike you as cheap now, and wholly inappropriate for an evening out.

This is supposed to be a vaguely hip restaurant, kind of a scene. You're going to stand out in this old blue sweater.

It's not old, you tell yourself. It's just plain. Simple. Not very trendy. But is it flattering? No, it's just a plain old sweater, not form-fitting, not interesting. There are some pills on it from washing. You tear it off and toss it in a garbage can on the sidewalk. It's July. You shouldn't have to wear a sweater. Though it can't be much more than sixty tonight. But no matter, you look better now. The black T-shirt is a few shades off from the pants, but inside, no one will be able to tell. You'll just look monochromatic. You can't go wrong with black. This is better. This is fine. You walk.

Is Delia going to end up with you? The ending of the book hinges on this question: if she's going to choose Graham and the life she has, or you and the life she wants. No wonder you're nervous. It's a very stressful situation. You're sort of hyperventilating. Not technically, but . . .

You stop, back up against the solid brick wall of a shoe store, and slowly inhale. Exhale. Inhale. Exhale. A man stops to ask if you're okay, but you shoo him away. You don't care what he thinks. He doesn't matter. Just filler, inconsequential.

The breathing helps—which is interesting, because you never believed that square breathing business would actually work—and so you hurry on. Five more blocks. It'll be fine. Just let yourself be guided by her. Don't come on too strong. But don't come on too loose. Or weak, rather. Didn't Corrone say that subtle is not always the best way?

The thing is to make her see the opportunity in you.

But you really want to know. The author has all this planned out, and you could do a much better job with your part if you knew for certain what would happen. "Are we going to end up together?" you ask the traffic light, the storefronts, the author.

A woman passing by gives you a strange look. This time you whisper. "If the light turns green in the next five seconds, then Delia has feelings for me. Okay? Just let me know."

And then the light turns green. You cross, excited but nervous. The author might be trying to confuse you. Maybe the light just happened to turn green. It has to turn green. And is the scratching still with you? You cover your ears to block out the putter of car motors and chatter of pedestrians. It's hard to tell, so you duck into a pub, but there's heavy metal playing on the stereo. People probably can't even hear each other talk. And though you hate to make yourself any later, a few seconds won't hurt. So you slip into the pharmacy next door. Much quieter here, and once the door chimes stop ringing, you can clearly hear the scratching of the pencil.

So this *is* going to be an important scene. "And she'll end up with me?" you whisper. What kind of answer do you expect? You're not sure. If yes, then the door will open in the next five seconds. Five, four, three, two, one. Door opens, enter old couple.

Wow. Kind of hard to trust the signs, but two for two isn't bad. You push past the old couple and head back outside. Three more blocks. And everything could be leading up to the ending you want. Which is the ending the reader wants. "Give them what they want," Corrone says. Of course the guy has to get the girl. You worry the whole time that it might not happen, but then at the last minute, it does. Nothing for the author to do but torture the reader, torture the characters, then follow through. It's like Corrone's *Island of No Tomorrows*. Near the end, sure, it looks like the hero is going to be decapitated by the islanders, but then it turns out that the unconscious girl they kicked off the bridge was actually the Slovenian spy he'd slept with in the middle of the book. You could tell from the adjectives of their lovemaking that they would be perfect together, and there, it all worked out in the end.

"All right, one more time," you whisper. If someone walks out of that place on the corner before you pass it, then she's in love with you. You walk hurriedly toward the end of the block, then slow your pace in case hurrying might interfere with the prediction. But the block seems so long, the answer so close at hand, that again you increase your stride, shoving through the crowd emerging from a bar, past a man on a cell phone pacing aimlessly in front of a restaurant. And just before you get to the corner, the door opens, remains opened for a moment, and then a man in a wheelchair rolls out onto the sidewalk. Does that count? "Are you fucking with me?" you all but shout. You turn to kick a wall, then stop yourself before pounding a foot into the brick. "Just make it happen," you whisper to the wall. "Make her love me. I've never asked you to do anything for me, and now I want you to do this. Okay?" You turn from the wall and walk on. "Okay?"

"Okay," says a dirty-looking man beside you. He reeks of smoke and liquor, but still, it feels like a sign. Kind of. It's so hard to be sure. You're a little chilly now. One more block. Should have kept the sweater for the walk.

Outside the restaurant, you stop for a moment to try to collect yourself. The thing is to get her to see the opportunity as a freedom. Or the other way around.

Someone giggles. "What?" she says.

It's Delia. She's standing beside you.

"I, um . . . nothing—I'm just thinking through something. The next chapter . . ."

"Okay," she says, and she nods. She's wearing a long black skirt and a black oxford shirt, and though you've seen them before, today they look less like a uniform and more like a suit of mourning. She's not wearing lipstick. Her hair is poking out from a bandanna, and she looks tired but, as always, beautiful. Her lips are still full and rosy without the makeup. "I put our name on the list," she tells you. "It should only be a few more minutes."

It's difficult to know how to interact with people whose friends or family members die. There are so many awkward pauses, so much how-are-you-doing and one-day-at-a-time. After a minute or two, the hostess seats you at a booth in the back corner. The walls in the restaurant are shockingly orange, but the brightness of the color is balanced by the dim lighting. A fern hangs above your head, and it reminds you of a fern hanging outside the door at Delia's father's house, but you push the memory out of your head. You both order, and she talks about her family and the funeral. You say "Oh," "Yeah," "Mmm hmm," and you listen. And the thing is to be helpful, to be the voice of reason, to be straightforward, not subversive.

"You're not going back to the foundation, are you?" you ask.

"I haven't even gotten that far. I have to deal with the house and . . ."

"If you want any help . . ."

The waitress arrives with your food, and so you wait while she sets down a colorful vegetable dish for Delia and burnt-smelling beef dish for you. You can't imagine eating anything, but you let a mushroom slither down your throat.

"I had to help deal with my grandfather's house once," you lie, "so I'd be glad to . . ."

"Thank you. I may take you up on that. I can't see Graham being a big help there, and Charlie had to go back to California."

"Any time," you say. That was good. Very good-friend behavior. Now just say it. Delia is picking at the broccoli with chopsticks. "So, I don't mean to be crass," you begin—and it already sounds crass, but you've started and she's listening and looking at you, so just get it out: "but I'm guessing you'll have a little more freedom—once everything's done."

"I guess so," she says. "I feel so trapped now, it's hard to think of it that way. You don't expect to have to plan a funeral when you're in your twenties. My aunt was such a godsend, and Monty's family. And now . . . well, at least circumstances have prevented me from suffering over whether or not to keep the house. There's no sentimental value left."

"I'm sure," you say. "And I know this has to be a terrible time and all, but it is finite, too. And then you'll have your whole life ahead of you and the freedom to do anything you want. *Anything*. No financial concerns for a while."

"Yeah."

"No ties to Boston," you venture.

This draws Delia's gaze from the mound of vegetables before her. "What do you mean?"

"Why not go to New York?" you say. "Audition. Do cabaret shows. Be the Delia who was singing Gershwin the other night."

She picks up a slice of carrot and smiles for the first time—but just for a second. "Well, Monty will be there," she says.

"Exactly," you say. "That'll make it easier. And I think I'll be moving there, too."

"*Really?*" she asks.

"Yes, really," you tell her. That one just came to you out of nowhere. Your own inspiration or the author's? There may not be much difference. "I've been working on a big project, Bank Rome, and it's based in New York. And, you know, Jon visits New York a lot. It could be great."

Delia doesn't say anything now as she sips a glass of water.

"Let me help you," you say. "It won't be that difficult. I promise. I don't think you have any idea how talented you are, and now you're free."

"I do need to do something," she says with a sigh. "But I don't know about right *now*. I'll have plenty of time once the house is dealt with, once I figure things out."

"What's to figure out? You've been wanting this for years, and now you don't have anyone to make you second-guess yourself, if you'll forgive my being blunt. You don't have financial concerns. The thing is . . ."

She looks at you as if you know what you're going to say.

"The thing is . . . you deserve to be appreciated."

She starts to cry. You move over to her side of the booth and hug her. She cries into your chest, reaches around and places a hand on your neck, and rubs a finger back and forth on your hairline. Right there in the restaurant. You almost kiss her, and you can tell that she almost kisses you. But it seems best to wait. Not to complicate the moment any further.

It was definitely the right line. You can almost hear the applause.

Delia

I THOUGHT YOU said it was a golden retriever," Delia calls to Graham through the bathroom door. He has the water on. Bastard. He's pretending not to hear, so she says it again.

The door opens a crack. "I must have been thinking of the other one," he tells her.

"So you walked *two* dogs this morning?" she asks, keeping her voice calm and pleasant, as her mother always did during arguments.

"Yes."

Delia walks into the kitchen and picks up half of a sandwich wrapped in waxed paper. Back on the sofa, she unwraps the sandwich on her lap, pulls out a thin slice of turkey, and offers it to Myra before picking out another slice for herself. "Well, I want to see them," she announces at length. "I think I'll go with you tonight."

"You can't." Graham walks up to the sofa and blocks the television. His hair is brushed, and he's wearing a clean shirt. In the mornings, he just rolls out of bed before he leaves, but he's been changing into clean clothes for his dog-walking nights.

"Why not?" Delia asks, dropping her gaze.

"We're not allowed to bring people into the houses."

Delia licks the mayonnaise off her fingers. "That's okay," she says. "I can wait outside while you get them."

"I have to water the plants and shit. I don't want you waiting outside in the dark for half an hour."

"Very thoughtful of you," she says, looking up at him now, "but I can bring one of the boys. They should be at Lilly's soon for martini night. We can pick them all up, make an evening of it."

Graham sits beside her and rolls a cigarette on the coffee table. She studies his face, but his eyes are concentrated on the paper and the tobacco. "Are you going to open the window?" she asks.

"Yeah, sorry," he says, then moves to the window and lights the cigarette.

"Unless," she adds, casting aside a tomato, "by 'walk a dog' you mean 'fuck a strange man for money.'" Graham starts to choke on his first inhale. "Could that be the problem?" she adds in the sweetest tone she can muster.

"What are you talking about?"

"I'm talking about yesterday afternoon," she snaps, abandoning the calm and pleasant plan. "When you were supposed to be out walking two, three, ten dogs, I passed you at the little coffee shop around the block. Where you were this morning, too. Funny how it takes so much longer when you walk the dogs at night."

"Delia—"

"I can't believe I bought that story. You never come back smelling like a dog. Myra never sniffs your clothes, there's no hair on them."

"Just—"

"And my goodness, you're always paid in cash. How long has this been going on, exactly? Was there *ever* a dog?"

Graham edges up to the sofa but stops short of sitting down. He sucks on his cigarette and blows the smoke behind him toward the window. "Delia, I *want* to stop," he tells her. "I did stop for a while. But you haven't been working and—"

"So now it's *my* fault? *I* made you do it? That's rich."

"That's not what I said," Graham tells her, moving back to the window to hold his cigarette outside. "I couldn't find another job."

"How hard did you look?" Delia starts fishing through the sandwich again, then tosses it onto the coffee table. "And *now*?" she says. "*Now* you're so worried about money? Daddy's finally giving me money, Graham! Your dream come true!"

She hates herself as the words come out.

"You know that's not true," he mumbles.

"I know," she says quietly.

"I was just trying to keep things covered until the estate is settled. It'll take some time, you know."

"Am I supposed to be grateful now?" Delia asks. "For the lying and the cheating and—"

"No, no, I'm just trying to explain, because—I love you, and as bad as this looks for me, I'm glad you know."

"Oh," Delia huffs, "how very big of you to be glad I caught you in a lie." Myra inches her bulk from the sofa to the table, and Delia swats the sandwich off the table and across the room. Graham stoops to pick it up, but she stops him. "I'll clean it up later."

Still, he starts gathering up the scattered pieces of sandwich.

"I said I'll clean it up!"

Graham puffs on his cigarette and returns to the window. Myra stares across the room at the abandoned food. Delia wraps herself in a quilt, knowing Myra's lethargy will prevail, and a moment later the cat settles down atop Graham's rolling papers on the coffee table. And then the silence is interrupted when Graham says, "I'm sorry I lied to you. And I'll stop, I promise. But I mean . . . when we first talked about this a while back, you seemed okay with it."

She was paralyzed, that's what she was. When he told her about what happened in New Orleans, how he'd gotten himself to Boston, how he'd rationalized it away. "I was never okay with it, Graham."

"You said you understood."

"—what you did when you were *sixteen*," she says, turning to face him, her voice suddenly hoarse. "We talked about this a thousand times, but there's no getting through to you. Finally I thought, fine, at worst you'd try it once and realize how insane it was. I didn't dream you'd like it."

For a rare moment, Graham is speechless. Then he says, "Delia, you know I'm not gay."

Delia drags her body off the sofa to pick up the sandwich and toss it into the trash. "What am I supposed to think?" she whispers. She's kneeling on the floor, only a few feet from Graham and a few moments from the end of the conversation she didn't realize she was going to have. "I love you, Graham. But you are a very sad, damaged person. And I don't know what it's going to take for you to fix your life. But I do know that this relationship . . . it can't be fixed anymore."

"You don't mean that," he says, but when he starts to put a hand on her shoulder, she shrugs him away and rises to her feet.

"No," she says, swallowing back the hesitation. "I do mean it. I'm too old to keep pretending . . ."

"No." His voice cracks. "No, listen, I saw Broadway Lady today. She was singing Sondheim again, 'We're Gonna Be All Right.' And I've been worrying about us, too, but I think we just need to listen to her and—"

"Broadway Lady is a mentally ill, drug-addicted homeless woman."

"No . . ." He stands there near the bedroom door, a tower of a man about to melt. And as Delia slides into her shoes and searches the sofa for her purse, she knows the look of helplessness on his face is going to haunt her. But his final words to her—"Is this about Daniel?"—give her the strength to move her body out the door.

MONTY AND JON have a cosmopolitan waiting for her when she reaches Lilly's, and immediately the story pours out. She recounts the argument without censorship, and Monty's shock and disgust register clearly on his face. "*How* could you have stayed with him?" he asks her. "Did you know about this?" he says to Jon.

"Oh, honey," Jon says, hugging her to his side.

Delia takes a sustaining sip of her drink before she can look Monty in the eyes. She doesn't need this tonight. "Let it go," she says. "He only did it for a few months, and it's over."

Monty lets out a dramatic sigh and downs the rest of his martini in one gulp.

"You're going to be okay, honey," Jon says. "And Graham will come out of this. He's going through a hard time."

"He's *trash*," Monty almost shouts.

Delia stares at him, but neither she nor Jon responds. Monty studies his empty glass for a moment, then says, "You're much too good for him. You know that, don't you?"

And she knows he's trying to be helpful, but the words sound so wrong.

"What are you thinking about doing?" Jon asks.

"Well," she says, "I think I might finally go to New York. Get away from everything, start fresh, and try to sing for real."

"That's wonderful," Monty says.

"You'll be moving there soon," she adds, "and Jon, you visit all the time. I can afford it now. So what's holding me back? It's like Daniel said—where is he, by the way?"

At first, neither of them says anything. Then they exchange a glance that makes Delia uneasy. Finally, Monty says, "We didn't call him." Jon just looks down at the table.

"I can call him," she says, reaching for her purse.

Jon pulls her in closer. "I don't think tonight's the night," he says.

"What's going on?" she asks.

Monty leans forward to rest his elbows on the table. "She might as well know," he says to Jon. "It turns out Daniel's a bit of a pathological liar."

"*Monty*," Jon hisses.

"Is this about the magazines again?" Delia asks.

"No, it's about the story he pulled off the Internet to read at my party."

"Ah, Natalie," Delia says, the name slithering through her teeth.

"She keeps up on these things. Reads a lot of the journals."

"She's so good at her work," Delia says, and she pulls away from Jon and reaches for her glass.

"There's no reason to get mad at her," Monty replies in an infuriatingly casual tone. "Or me for that matter. I just thought you should know that he's not a writer at all."

"Now, we don't know that," Jon says.

"No, you don't," she tells them. "Maybe he's afraid to read his stuff in front of everyone. It's hard to get up in front of people. He doesn't even know us that well."

"No, he doesn't," Monty says pointedly. "And we don't know him."

"Jon?"

She doesn't even know what the question is, but when she turns to him, he starts to shake his head. "Honey, you know I think he's a nice guy, but he is kind of strange. But it doesn't matter anymore, right? He's been fun for the summer, and you're going to New York."

"So is he," she says. And this statement provokes inexplicable looks of horror from both of them. "I've read his novel," she tells them. "It's very good. Clever, interesting, suspenseful." She's lying, but the fiction isn't having as strong a reaction as she'd hoped.

"*Why* is Daniel moving to New York?" Jon asks.

"For work," she says. "Some Italian bank—"

"Bank Rome?" Monty asks, and she nods. "Bank Rome is at least three years away from opening up in the U.S. At least."

"He's working on the plans," Delia tells him.

"So was I," Monty says. "But I won't be anymore, because that account is based in Boston. Not in New York."

Why are they doing this, she wants to ask. Why can't they leave her alone? Monty doesn't know everything. Maybe Daniel just feels like moving. Or he's going to another firm. Or maybe he just wants to be with her. She almost says this, but she can't. Her throat is suddenly so tight, her body hot all over.

"Honey, don't you think Daniel might be trying a little *too* hard, might be just a little *too* helpful?"

"You know, I can think of worse things," Delia says, and she grabs her purse and slides out of the booth in one movement. "Thank you both for your heartfelt concern. But I don't need any more advice. I know what I'm doing."

Outside the fresh air greets her like a tonic, and Delia can feel the oxygen replenishing her body as she hurries down Massachusetts Avenue toward the Porter Square Station. She doesn't know what she's doing this minute, but she knows what she's doing in life. Putting the past behind her. And that includes all condemnations—from her father and Graham, Monty, now even Jon. She's tired of being dragged down and weighed down and treated like a child. Maybe Daniel has a few things to explain. But he believes in her. That might not be enough for forever, but it counts for a lot right now.

Daniel

NEITHER OF YOU speaks when she first arrives. Her eyes are red, her cheeks stained with tears, and you hold her in a tight embrace that feels poignant. Before leaving the threshold of your apartment, she tells you that she's left Graham, and you rub her back and tell her it will be okay. Then you lead her to the table, and she tells you that Graham hasn't stopped hustling, and you want to drop to your knees and blow kisses at the sky. But instead you listen calmly and put a hand on Delia's shoulder and play your part. And it makes sense, when you think about it. That must be where the author has been for the past few days. Tracking Graham's demise. Creating it.

"It's really over this time," she says.

It's so clean, so perfect. First, he turns down the auditions—that was a test—and now, at the turning point of her life, he's showing his potential. This is all he can do. He's all wrong for her.

You carefully maneuver through her questions to give the

answers she seems to want. Yes, she had to leave Graham. And yes, Monty was terribly insensitive about it. He has no right to judge her. And yes, Graham will be okay on his own. And she will, too. And yes, yes, she should move to New York. You have so much you want to say, but you don't. Instead, you're guided by her through the conversation and then guided by her to the bedroom, where she strips down to a gray T-shirt and a pair of pink underwear and asks you to hold her.

All night you lie with her, your chest to her back, your arms around her waist, your hands warming her cold fingers. You listen to her breathing, the author's pencil scratching. And in the half-wakefulness of dawn, your movements are wholly natural and organic: your fingertips against her arm, her palm on your thigh, your hand under her shirt, a kiss on the back of her neck. She rolls onto her back, her hands trace the sides of your body. The build-up is long and uncomplicated and dreamlike. And when your few articles of clothing are shed, there's no need for you to escape to the bathroom or question the author's intentions. You and she make love like two people in love, two people who desperately need each other. Like two people ending a book happily ever after. You are deep inside her, inside her body and mind and heart. She pants, says "oh" every few minutes, and you watch her face tense and release. You try to picture the movie version of the book and wonder how this scene will unfold, what the soundtrack might be, if you should have turned on music, but then you push the thoughts out of your mind. You are what she needs, and you know she knows that. You'll take care of her in every way. "I love you," you tell her. "I love you."

Afterward, she lies with her head on your chest, and for a long time you brush your fingers through her hair. You're not sure if she's awake, but then she asks, "Would you be moving to New York if it weren't for me?"

Your hesitation lasts only a moment. "No," you tell her, and you know this is the right answer because she nuzzles her cheek against your chest and holds tight to your body. You ask her what you should bring to her first show, roses or lilies or maybe . . . what do orchids look like, you ask, and she laughs. You can't bring a bouquet of orchids, she tells you. Maybe you'll try, you say. Where will you take her to dinner after her Broadway debut? Somewhere fancy? Or a little dive someplace where no one can find you? "Mmm, I'm hungry now," she tells you. And reluctantly, you both peel yourselves out of bed.

She sits in your bathrobe while you make the eggs and coffee, while you slice the apples and make toast. You kiss her quickly behind the ear before sitting down. "I'm glad you're here," you tell her.

"Me too," she says.

"And I'm glad you want to move to New York. How much do you have to do before you can leave?"

"Well," she says, "I don't think the foundation truly expects me to come back. And I guess there's no rush to go through the house until the lawyer says we're free to put it on the market. I don't know why it's so complicated to settle an estate. Aside from a few charities, it's just Charlie and me. Dad didn't have much debt, and not much was taken in the robbery—except my mother's jewelry, which is really sad. I used to play dress-up with some of that stuff. Dad would get so mad," she adds, laughing to herself, "but my mother thought it was a riot. Me wearing her high heels and a big emerald brooch out in the backyard. . . . I always imagined I'd wear that brooch to the Tonys one day or in Carnegie Hall. To have a piece of Mom with me. I guess they're just things, though."

"Well, you wanted to sell most of it, right?" you ask.

"Oh, no," she tells you. "I could never have done that."

"But I thought you said . . ."

"No, that was just talk." She's not eating, just sipping coffee and staring into the air. You should say something now. Something sympathetic and caring.

"More coffee?" you ask.

"Sure," she says.

That was heartwarming. You pour her another cup and sit down again.

"We could get a place together, if you want," you say without looking up. "I don't mean to be presumptuous. Just for starters, to see how—"

"Yeah," she says. "That would be good."

This is all being written. Being written just the way you hoped it would be. You've stopped buttering your toast, your hands frozen midair in a foolish pose. Like you're a mime. So you make the limbs continue to move, force down a dry wedge.

"Can I ask you a question?" she asks—in a way that worries you, but you say of course. "I feel funny bringing this up," she continues, "but . . . that story you read at Monty's party. You didn't write it, did you?"

This is unexpected, and after a pause—brief but still too long—you can only manage to say, "What?"

"Natalie found it online," Delia continues, and you can feel her gaze cutting through your forehead. You look down at the lines of egg yolk running across your plate and onto the tablecloth. "It's okay, Daniel. You don't need to try to impress me. It's okay if you're not a published author, it is. But I want to know the truth. Was that your story?"

"No," you say. It's painful, but the word comes out safely. You'll work it out. It's going to be okay. She's looking you in the eye. She seems fine.

"And is there really a novel?" she asks.

That one's harder. A second passes. Two. More.

Then, "Yes," you tell her. "Yes. There is a book."

She studies you for a minute, and you can feel yourself start to sweat, but you don't wipe your forehead, don't want to call attention to it. Delia looks down at her toast, then up again, and says, "Can I see it?"

"No."

"Why not?"

"It's not finished."

"That's okay."

"But I can't show it to you. It's very . . ." You search your mind for a word, tour your memory of Corrone's manual. You need a word that sounds authorial. You need a word like—"raw," you say. "It's very raw. I'd be embarrassed."

She nods, but it's not a sympathetic-looking nod. Her eyes look distant, guarded, maybe even distrustful. You stand up and go to the refrigerator to steal a minute to think. Why is the author doing this? Everything was going so well. You take out a jar of blueberry preserves and slowly sift through the utensil drawer to find a long spoon. She thinks you're lying. She has some cause to think so. But it's not good for you.

When you find the spoon and stop shuffling utensils around, you can hear that the scratching has moved further way. It's no longer above you or in the kitchen. You turn, but Delia is still seated behind you. What's happening, you wonder. Without meeting her eyes, you follow the sound into the living room. The scratching hovers in the room, hovers over your desk in fact, over—yes—the Corrone manual and your brainstorming notebook. You grab both and bring them into the kitchen, where Delia drops her gaze from your face to the books in your hand.

"I don't want you to read any of this," you begin, "but—" You thumb through the notebook quickly, flipping past page after page of your marketing notes. You don't pause long enough for her to read anything. You just want to prove that you have written many words. "See," you say. "And here's a book about writing, and—" Stuffed into the Corrone manual are a few printouts. Of what? False starts on your story for salon night. See, you kept these for a reason! You flip to the first page. " 'It was late at night when Detective Mahoney walked into the bureau,' " you read. "It's just crap, but . . ."

Delia seems to be loosening up. She nods. She believes you. "So," she says, "it's a detective story?"

"No," you say, "that was just something that didn't work out."

"It's a love story?"

"Yeah, I hope."

"That's great. And what's your character's name? Just so I can say I know something about it, if anyone asks."

"Um . . ." This shouldn't be hard, but your mind is blank. Why didn't you just stick with Detective Mahoney and be done with it? It was a perfectly fine name. This isn't difficult. How about— "Thorgon."

Delia smiles now. "*Thorgon?*" she says, with the beginning of a laugh. "I'm sorry, I don't mean to make fun, but your main character is named *Thorgon?*"

"Not my *main* character. Just someone who, you know, someone who appears at some point in there."

Delia stands and walks up to you. She rubs your head for a second. "Thank you," she says. "Monty and Jon said they thought you weren't writing a book at all, but I defended you."

She defended you. That was just written. You can hear the pencil scratching around you. "Well," you say, "there is a book."

"I know," she says, and she stands on her tiptoes and kisses you on the forehead.

The sigh in your head is so much bigger than any sigh you could let out in front of her. Or on the page, even. You hope you've been coming across as a little more confident than you've been feeling. Because this is the homestretch. She wants to live with you. She defended you. This is awesome. Whew. Okay, yes, this is awesome.

You return the notebook and Corrone manual to your desk, then go to clean up the kitchen. Delia dries dishes while you wash. You talk about New York sublets. You talk about Brooklyn versus Manhattan, Hell's Kitchen versus Greenwich Village. It's expensive, she says, but then so is Boston, you both agree. You turn on the computer and start searching for sublets together, and after a little while, she prints out a few promising ads and starts making calls, and you leave to take the first shower.

The scratching follows you. It must be loud, or maybe you're listening for it extra carefully. But it's there. The book goes on. And where will the final moment take place? Packing up the car, perhaps. Taking off on the highway. Maybe at your new apartment in New York, with you opening the door for Delia, just like you did so many times that night you first met. That would be a nice—what's the word? repetition?—*echo* of the earlier scene.

You towel off quickly. You throw on a pair of blue jeans and a T-shirt. And when you walk back into the living room to find out how Delia's calls went, you see her seated at the computer holding your notebook.

"This is all about Vector Microsystems," she says to you. "And Bank Rome. There are grocery lists in here, Daniel. If this is the raw material for a novel, it's pretty fucking boring."

"Delia—"

"God, what is it about me that makes people want to lie to me?" She's standing, holding your notebook, looking into you, through you. "I'm serious," she says. "I'd like to know."

Why is this happening? Why would you have put the note-book right back on the desk? You should've hidden it. Why would the author have made you do that? Now you have to do something. You have to fix this. Maybe—no, you can't. But maybe you should. Yes, let the truth reveal itself, says a voice in your head. Is it your conscience speaking or the author? You can't be sure, they could be the same thing. Tell her, says the voice. It'll be okay. And you can't just keep standing here, be-cause there's that incredulous look on her face, and a few min-utes ago she wanted to move to New York with you, to love you. You need to say it. You can picture the words in your mind, underlined, scrawled in the margin. This is the scene where Daniel says—

"We're in a book."

As soon as the words come out, you know that they're not sufficient. They confuse before they can simplify. "I mean, there really is a book," you tell her. "It's just that we're in it. It's being written. As we stand here."

Still, Delia doesn't seem to follow. You need to explain with-out upsetting her any further. But it's important that she under-stand. She'll be so relieved when she understands.

"I know it sounds weird," you say in your most soothing tone. "But we're actually in a book, and the reason I know this is be-cause I can hear the author—well, the pencil, actually. I can hear when the author is writing because I can hear the pencil. Which most people can't hear, I don't think. Can you hear it? Listen."

In the pause, there is nothing but Delia's wide eyes, the rum-ble of a car passing outside, and the scratching of the pencil.

"Hear what?"

"Scratching. In the air."

Delia's eyes narrow. What does that mean? It doesn't look good. "No," she says. "I can't hear anything."

"I know it sounds far-fetched. It took me the longest time to come to terms with it."

"So, you're *in* a book?"

"You are, too," you say. "We all are. We're just not always on the page. The author comes and goes, picks up the story and then drops it—like a book, of course. But we're on the page right now. This whole thing is being written. This whole conversation. Take a sip of coffee."

Delia stares at you, motionless.

"Go ahead. Please."

Slowly, she reaches back to the desk for her mug, takes a small sip, then sets it down again. She doesn't take her eyes off you.

"See, that was written. The author was writing the whole time."

Delia doesn't speak at once. Then, slowly, she says, "So all this time, you haven't been writing a book, you've been in one?" She speaks in a matter-of-fact tone. She's starting to get it.

"Exactly," you say. "I thought it was your book at first, that maybe I'd just popped into it," you explain, "but now I think it's *our* book." You can't suppress the proud grin. "I'm sorry for lying to you. I'm not really an artist, I know. But I do sort of have a gift. It's just a different kind."

"What's the book about, Daniel?"

It's a lot for her to take in, you know. "It's about us falling in love," you say. "At first, I thought it was going to be about how a new person came along and helped all of you realize your dreams and make it big, but then Graham didn't want to go on the auditions, and Jon was a little discouraging."

She's nodding a little bit now. "You got Monty the promotion, didn't you?" she says.

"I just wanted to help make something happen. You're all smart and funny and talented, and you have these exciting dreams, but no one was doing much about them. And in a book, people have to do things and they have to change. You can't stay the same throughout the story. But now with Monty moving to New York, and now us, it's so obvious. This is the book of personal change. The Boston book, the coming-of-age book, the love story. The *sequel* will be about success." The idea just occurred to you suddenly. But Corrone says a writer with commercial promise should always set up a sequel, and that must be what's happening. "The next book is going to be the New York story," you tell her. "Your rise to fame. Making your Carnegie Hall debut with the emerald brooch and all."

"I don't *have* the brooch, Daniel," she almost shouts.

"I know, but I do."

You shouldn't have said that. Why did you say that? You didn't even feel the words forming in your mind. Or *inserted* in your mind. Pushed in and out all in one stroke.

"Oh my God," Delia is mumbling, her hands rising to her face. "Oh my God."

You have to fix this. You're dumping it out much too quickly. And all around you the persistent scraaaatching.

"It was totally not what I expected," you tell her. "I was just trying to get you that jewelry. To make you self-sufficient. You said it was yours, and I figured if it was stolen, you wouldn't have to worry about arguing with your father about it. But I was going to leave it up to you. We could have put it back. But then he came home and things got out of hand—"

"I told you exactly where to find the gun," she says, her eyes falling to the table.

"But the author made you do that. It's not like you were telling me to go and shoot—and I didn't want that either. Believe me, that wasn't my plan. But I guess the author figured that if your father was out of the picture, you could . . ."

Shut up. You've got to calm her down. Her eyes are red, she's chewing on her bottom lip, she's starting to cry. She's freaking. So you hurry to your bedroom and pull out the jewelry box from the suitcase beneath your bed. She has her clothes in her hands when you return to the living room. She takes the box from you and clutches it to her chest, but she doesn't open it. "I've got to go," she says.

"No," you tell her, "no, you don't understand. This is just what happened. I know it's sad, but now you're free. It's nobody's fault."

There are tears in her eyes. She won't look at you.

"We're still going to New York?" you ask her.

Delia bites her lip and nods.

"Where are you going?"

"To . . . to get some things."

"Let me help you," you say. "Graham might not be nice. And you're upset." She seems so overwhelmed and fragile. But so tender, too.

"No, I'll be fine."

"I love you," you say again. Show, don't tell. Show her. You reach for her waist and pull her toward you to remind yourself what the kiss felt like, to remind her. But her mouth is weak against yours, her tongue limp.

"Daniel, I have to go," she says again.

Up close like this, you can see the brown roots in her hair. She's still wearing your bathrobe, and in a way, she doesn't look much older than the little girl you saw in the photograph at her father's house.

"Let me go," she says. "Please. I won't tell."

"I'm not sure if you understand," you say, and you loosen your grip, but you're not ready for her to leave.

"I do," she says. "I understand." She meets your gaze for a second, her eyes red and dark and moist.

"You're just going to get some stuff?"

"Yes, I promise," she says, pulling herself away from your hold. "I won't be long," she adds. And then she grabs her purse from the sofa, tugs her clothes on, and hurries out the door and down the stairs. Without saying she loves you too.

For a minute you stand there looking at the open door, listening to the scratching around you, and wondering if everything has fallen apart. The author might have switched gears on you at the last minute. It might be possible.

But no, this is just how books work. The last-minute crisis before everything turns out the way you hope it will. It's like Corrone's first Mafia novel. You want Alfonso to end up with Carla the whole time, but then, right near the end, there's that scene with the meat slicer, and it's like there's no way she could have made it, blood all over the page. But then, sure enough, after Alfonso kills his brother, he finds Carla hiding in the bakery, and it turns out she only lost two fingers, not even important ones.

So it's like you and Delia—only not as gory. Right now it seems possible that things might not work out, but they will. She has a lot to digest, sure, but it was hard for you, too, when you first understood what the scratching meant. She'll be back. She feels the connection. She's the one who seduced you, way back when. She's the one who came to you last night. The happy resolution will come. The author has to save something for the final scene.

———

HOURS LATER, YOU stand before your open closet door plucking out dress shirts to give to Goodwill. You toss two onto the bed beside a pile of sweaters and old polo shirts, then quickly add two more. You're probably going to have to get a small place in New York, no room for junk. Monet is going, as is half your wardrobe. You've already e-mailed your resume to a few headhunters in New York and to the bank VP who seemed so impressed with your last presentation. You should be able to sublet your apartment if you can't get out of the lease. Get rid of most of the furniture, too.

She's not angry, you say to yourself for the millionth time. She wanted you to be honest—she deserves your honesty. She told you about Graham; it's only fair for you to be honest with her. It'll be better for your relationship in the long run. And she won't tell the guys. It would be so awkward, and how could she explain it—the book, the author? She won't say anything. She needs you.

You hold up a pair of slacks you don't recognize, then slip off your jeans to try them on. Too baggy, not flattering at all. So you add the slacks to the stack on the bed, and then try on another pair. These are okay, but a little loose.

She's taking a while, but the scratching has just returned, so you figure she'll be here any minute. The author probably followed her to write the last farewell scene with Graham. You can see him shouting insults, Delia defending you. That's what must have taken her so long.

You wonder if the sequel will pick up immediately or begin later. Maybe it'll start after you and Delia are settled in New York. Monty and Natalie will probably get married in the meantime. Maybe you should, too. No, better to save it for the sequel. Jon could be in the next book, too. He might rethink things, might see Delia making it and decide to give acting another shot. You'll have a new set of artistic friends: actors and singers and writers and—maybe you should try writing a novel. Now that you know how it works. It takes a lot more planning than you thought, planting the seeds and watering the garden and all that, but now that you've been through one pretty much start to finish, you should be able to pull it off. Just start. And once you get started, you can't stop. That's what Corrone says. This is perfect. She'll like that.

The corduroys look pretty nice. Why don't you ever wear these, you wonder, slipping them off and putting them back on the hanger.

Pacing into the kitchen, you allow yourself to worry for a moment that Delia might not return. It is possible. Though everything points toward a happy ending. You pull out a loaf of bread and can of tuna fish from the pantry. The mayonnaise might be bad, you think, opening the refrigerator door. "If she's on her way back, then the mayonnaise is spoiled." You wait a beat and glance into the living room. "Okay?" you say. But you don't wait for a response. You unscrew the jar, and it only takes one whiff for you to know your future. You'll be making love again tonight. Sooner, perhaps. Any time now.

As if in reply, you hear a noise outside. A car door. She came by train before—but of course, she had to drive back to bring all her stuff. You should have thought of that. You should have insisted on helping. From the living room window, you can't see her, but there's usually more parking on the other side of the house. You listen carefully for the author. Pencil is still scratching—and more rapidly, if you're not mistaken. Footsteps on the stairs. Your heart is racing now. One book at a time, and this one's about to end. This is one of those moments that you think will never come but then actually does.

But you're prepared. Just be calm, you tell yourself, controlling your stride to the living room. Wait for her to knock.

A quick rap on the door follows almost instantly on this thought, and you take a deep breath. It's all happened so fast. Already, the final love scene. Slowly, you reach for the door-knob, braced for the kiss that will greet you.

Acknowledgments

A WORLD OF THANKS to my agent, Bill Clegg, and my editor, Marjorie Braman, for being such insightful readers and enthusiastic advocates. Thanks also to everyone at Harper Perennial and the William Morris Agency.

Many thanks to three terrific professors, Wilton Barnhardt, Angela Davis-Gardner, and John Kessel, for their invaluable guidance as I developed this book. Thanks also to everyone else who suffered through drafts and revisions, especially Tommy Jenkins, Penelope Robbins, Jodi Lynn Villers, and Brent Winter.

I want to thank two of the most important writing teachers I had growing up, Linda Hobson and Doris Betts. I am also grateful to the Weymouth Center for the Arts & Humanities for offering me such a beautiful place to work, and to Virginia Barber, David Ferriero, Chris Hildreth, John

Piva, Sheila Smith McKoy, and Peter Vaughn for their help along the way.

Finally, let me thank my most biased supporters: Mom and Dad, Allison and Nancy, Granny and Aunt Betsy, Jean and Rachel, and Austin, who keeps me smiling.

About the author

About the book

Read on

Insights,
Interviews
& More . . .

Meet William Conescu

Chris Hildreth

WILLIAM CONESCU was born in New York and raised in New Orleans. He graduated from the University of North Carolina at Chapel Hill and earned an MFA in creative writing at North Carolina State University. His short stories have appeared in *The Gettysburg Review*, *New Letters*, *Green Mountains Review*, and other publications. *Being Written* is his first novel.

William lives in Chapel Hill, North Carolina. You can visit him online at www.williamconescu.com. ⟳

Do You Write with a Pencil?
(and other important information)

Do you write with a pencil?

I generally write my first drafts on the computer. But when I revise, I sit down with a hard copy of the manuscript and scribble all over it in pencil.

Favorite places to write?

In my home office with my two cats sleeping nearby. I've also gone on a few writing retreats, which can be great.

Daytime or nighttime?

Either, but never terribly early in the morning or late at night.

Fuel required?

Coffee, Sno-Caps or dark chocolate M&Ms, and Orbit sweet mint-flavored gum. (Fancy taste, I know.)

First people to see your drafts?

I'm in a writers group with some friends who were in my MFA program.

Most annoying interruptions?

I like it to be pretty quiet when I write. Lately, I've been having to tune out a suicidal bird that keeps thrusting itself into my window. I'm a vegetarian, but I'm having second thoughts. ∾

The Author Is Interviewed by a Minor Character from His Novel

Jennifer: I read your little book.

William: Thank you.

Jennifer: I'm barely in it. I have three lines on page 22.

William: Yes, I know.

Jennifer: And I did not have "spherical hair" that day.

William: It looked pretty spherical to me.

Jennifer: It was curled under. My roommate said it looked cute.

William: Okay, I'm sorry. . . . So are you really here to interview me?

Jennifer: Of course I'm here to interview you. Now tell me, Mr. Conescu, how did the idea for *Being Written* come to you?

William: Well, my story ideas often begin with a scenario. In this case, I started out thinking it would be fun to write about a guy who knows he's in a novel, but he's the equivalent of a movie extra. He's a warm body. He fills out crowd scenes. If a novel calls for someone sitting at a table across the room or passing on the sidewalk, my guy could be that guy.

Jennifer: And you felt that Daniel Fischer was the best choice? There weren't other minor characters—women, perhaps, with spherical hair—who might have made better choices?

William: Daniel did have this awareness that he was a character. That was kind of key.

> 66 If a novel calls for someone sitting at a table across the room or passing on the sidewalk, my guy could be that guy. 99

Jennifer: Of course. Yet you did manage to write plenty of lines for characters who, like me, did not realize they were in a novel. Let's talk about the "artsy" social circle that Daniel enters. Where did those characters come from?

William: They weren't based on me or on anyone in particular, but they emerged from a world that I was part of—people who were active in the arts in college and in the years that followed but then, as time passed and bills had to be paid, shifted gears for any number of reasons.

Jennifer: Do you think that kind of gear-shifting is common among writers and actors and musicians?

William: I do, but I don't think it's unique to people in the arts. A lot of people in their twenties and thirties are stumbling into new professions and taking some time to figure out what they want to do and who they want to be.

Jennifer: Do you have any musical or acting talents we should know about?

William: Not really. I did some acting in college. I only had two lines in my first show, but they gave me three costumes, a fat suit, and a haircut. I felt very important. Then there were the requisite high school musicals.

Jennifer: Such as?

William: I played Cornelius in *Hello, Dolly!* Joe Hardy, the baseball player, in *Damn Yankees*. That's the closest I came to lettering in a sport.

Jennifer: Now tell me, have you considered, by any chance, basing your next novel on the minor character Jennifer and her strained relationship with her mother? ▶

> "I did some acting in college. I only had two lines in my first show, but they gave me three costumes, a fat suit, and a haircut."

The Author Is Interviewed by a Minor Character from His Novel (*continued*)

William: No.

Jennifer: Do you want to hear about it?

William: No.

Jennifer: I've been journaling about it lately. Do you want to read my journals?

William: No.

Jennifer: All right, moving on . . . All of the chapters that are written from Daniel's perspective are written in the second person. When you first conceived of the novel, did you know you wanted to write it this way?

William: No, not at all. The first few chapters went through many forms, and I wrote a complete draft in the third person. But something was missing. I needed more tension between Daniel's sections and the rest of the book. Then it occurred to me to try out the second person, and that immediately felt right. Through the second person, I was able to show Daniel's perception of being written into a book. Then through the other chapters, I could let the reader see "the book" itself, and I could show what the other characters thought of Daniel's presence. Of all the changes that took place during the writing process, this was the most important. And the most fun.

Jennifer: Well, thank you for talking with me today. I think that just about concludes this interview. I would like to add for the record that I was nothing but nice to Delia—

William: I know.

Jennifer: —and she had no cause to dislike me.

William: I know. I tell you what, Jennifer. I'll talk to my publisher, and I'll see if we can put a transcript of this interview in the back of my book. That way you'll have plenty of lines.

Jennifer: You'd do that for me?

William: Sure.

Jennifer: Can you say that I have long auburn locks that fall just below my shoulders?

William: But you don't.

Jennifer: I know, but I've been thinking about growing my hair out.

William: Okay, sure. We'll say that.

"Blind"
A Short Story

"Blind" was first published in the Green Mountains Review *(vol. 20, 2007) and is reprinted by courtesy of the author.*

THE FIRST MORNING I was blind, I called in sick. My boss's secretary took the message.

The second morning I was blind, she said, *Yeah, something's going around the office.*

The third morning I was blind, she asked if I could check my e-mail from home. I said I'd see if I could later on. Then I coughed a few times and hung up.

I stayed in bed a lot those first few days. What with all the bumping into and stepping on, it just felt safer—plus I ran out of Band-Aids pretty quickly. I watched movies and news programs on TV—well, listened to them anyway. I'd flip the pages of a magazine to keep my hands busy. I thought about working on the blanket I'd been knitting for my niece, but then I thought better of it.

After a week of being blind, I figured it wasn't a cold. Or a headache. Or something a new pair of glasses could fix. I stopped calling into the office. I felt bad—the election was coming up—but then how bad could I feel, really? After another week, my boss called me. He was worried-slash-angry. I said something about being sick, and he said something about respect and rights and disabilities and world order. Then he said something about mailing me some forms to have my doctor fill out. Maybe he did. I haven't seen them.

At some point I switched to soaps and talk shows. They were easier to follow and easier to imagine. Every woman on a soap looks like she just stepped out of a beauty parlor, and

> " After a week of being blind, I figured it wasn't a cold. Or a headache. Or something a new pair of glasses could fix. "

people on talk shows tend to be fat and poorly groomed. I'd half-listen. I'd brush my hair. Braid it, unbraid it. I painted my nails once. I used to paint my nails most Sunday mornings, but it felt odd not knowing what the color was now, so I took it off before it had time to dry.

I drank sodas and orange juice and ate cheese and sandwich meat. Things in boxes and bags, things that didn't require a stove or an oven. Cereal. It was fine. It was like being a man. Canned soup. Microwave dinners. I ate things I don't remember buying. Could've been years old. Frozen meats I couldn't identify. It's a very economical way to clean out the kitchen. You can't suffer over whether or not something looks good or has passed the expiration date. If it's there and smells okay, then you can put ketchup on it and eat it. When I ran out of ketchup, I used some other thing. It wasn't barbecue sauce. I'm not sure what it was.

When the kitchen was pretty much empty, except for oregano and cooking spray, I called information and got the number for the pizza-and-subs place around the corner. That was a nice change. I paid in cash for as long as I could, just handed the delivery boy most of the bills from my wallet and took back the change.

(*Um, this is four dollars.*

Oh, I thought I gave you a ten. I must be blind. Here.

Um, this is another one.

Whoops. Silly me.)

When I was down to all ones, I handed the boy a credit card. He said you usually have to give the number over the phone, but he'd write it down this once. I said, *Thanks, things have been a little crazy lately*, and he said, *Yeah, I know how it is.*

I figure it's either a brain tumor, a ▶

stroke, or some horrible disorder. I don't really need to know which. Whatever the case, it's kind of a shame I quit smoking those last three times, because I'll probably die before lung cancer would've gotten me. Then again, maybe it's just as well that I don't smoke now. I still don't remember where the matches are, and besides, it's not a good idea for blind people to play with fire.

I struggled to remember where a lot of things were in those early weeks. Like the end tables, the electrical outlets, the path to the front door. Paper towels, sugar, tampons, the cord for the electric razor. Tampons. I washed my sheets twice in a row just in case. I think I used bleach.

After a month or so—it's hard to keep track—I was out of food and cash. I'd raided my change drawer, pulled out all the quarters and dimes. I had no idea where my checkbook was. So finally, I ordered something from the pizza-and-subs place like usual, but when the boy arrived, I told him it was no big deal, but I'd give him a twenty-dollar tip or my laptop or a hand job if he'd help me memorize my credit card number. He said that was cool. He had to be back at work soon, so he'd just take the twenty dollars.

He was pretty easygoing. We spent about ten minutes on it, and I gave him the tip plus a few magazines, *Newsweek*s or something, I'm not sure. He'd commented on them— they were on the coffee table, apparently— and what was I going to do with them? Before he left, I explained to him the whole blind thing. He said, yeah, he had his suspicions.

The power was the first to go off. (*Really, you sent a bill? I'm sitting at my desk, and*

> 66 Then again, maybe it's just as well that I don't smoke now. I still don't remember where the matches are, and besides, it's not a good idea for blind people to play with fire. 99

I don't see it anywhere.) The mortgage people were next. (*I've been sick, shut in. Can you take a credit card over the phone?*) You never want to become blind without a credit card. I made up a little song in my head to be sure I wouldn't forget the number.

I tried to learn the order of people in my cell phone directory, too. I called my way down the list. I'd see who answered, then hang up or say hello. But I didn't make it past *N*, because it gets tiresome listening to people complain. My cousin was having marriage trouble again. My old college roommate was worried about the president. My mother fussed about her allergies and her asthma, and my ex-husband was stressing about his coffee shop franchise in Houston. When people asked, I'd say things with me were fine. I'd say, *Can't complain*, in that little singsongy way. People like it when you say, *Can't complain.*

Oh, well, that's goooood, they always say. Every time.

The pizza-and-subs boy sold my car. He helped clear a better path for me through the living room. He had furry cheeks. And earrings in his left ear and left nostril. And an eagle tattooed on his forearm, or so he said. He got big tips every time. He said he was glad to help. He said it was a bum rap. He said my roots were showing big-time, and did I know how retarded I looked wearing plaid with stripes?

Shopping is tricky when you're blind. There's some guesswork involved, some awkwardness. Ordering a dozen solid blue shirts is not as simple as you'd think it should be. (*Actually, I don't have the catalog in front of me. No, Internet's down. So it was dark blue. Okay cobalt, sure. V-neck, okay,* ▶

> ❝ When people asked, I'd say things with me were fine. I'd say, *Can't complain,* in that little singsongy way. People like it when you say, *Can't complain.* ❞

*sounds right. And then there was, um, another
blue shirt—yes, one more, still blue . . .)*
Thankfully, I remembered the name of a
woman I used to work with who once asked
me to accept Jesus as my personal savior, then
tried to get me to sign up for a multilevel
marketing program. She said she was glad
to hear from me. They missed me at the
office. I asked her to ship me toiletries and
tampons and nonperishable foods—she only
sells one brand of everything, which makes
shopping easier. She asked me if I wanted to
go with her to church one day soon. I said I'd
think about it, and she said she'd pray for me
to feel better, and then I told her someone
was at the door and I had to go.

Every time the pizza-and-subs delivery
boy came over, he'd take something. Another
magazine. The alarm clock. A vase—his
sister's birthday was coming up. We'd have
sex sometimes. He'd skim through my mail,
take the trash out to the curb. I think he was
a virgin.

When you turn blind, at some point, your
mother's bound to find out.

(*Why didn't you tell me?*
It didn't come up. How's Tiger?)
She was annoyed, I know. She felt left out.
There were a lot of questions. (*You couldn't
water the plants? Look at this—the ficus is
unsalvageable.*) There was a lot of sympathy.
She tweezed my eyebrows. She dyed my hair
back to brown. She said I needed to start
shaving my legs. She gave me some money.
The six doctors she called had six different
explanations and wanted to do six different
tests. I stopped paying attention after she told
me about the first two.

Fruit baskets came. And came. And came.
And baskets of cheeses. I'd ask the pizza-and-

> ❝ Thankfully,
I remembered
the name of a
woman I used to
work with who
once asked me to
accept Jesus as my
personal savior,
then tried to get
me to sign up
for a multilevel
marketing
program. ❞

subs delivery boy to read me the names. They all tasted strong and white and bitter. People sent over dinners and yarn and scented candles. Scented candles aren't relaxing when you're blind.

Money started coming in, too. My mother filled out some papers. I guess she deposited the checks; it all seemed to work out. I started shaving with the electric razor. I got my mom to cut my hair so it would be easier to deal with. And I asked the boy to move in with me.

It made sense. He saved money on rent. And there was space. One weekend, we went through everything, all of my clothes, furniture, closets. Just cleaned things out. Everything glass—the dishes, the coffee table—gone. Everything inessential—knickknacks, books, pictures he didn't like. And he was nice to have around. (*Watch that corner. You missed a button. Here, touch this.*)

Life became so easy after that. We'd listen to music together, or he'd watch one of his movies. At night, he'd play video games, and I'd nod off to the sound of electronic car chases or gunfire or a digital girl shouting *Help me, Help me* on the television set. Sometimes we played two-player. I'd shoot randomly or push buttons when he told me to. He'd carry the game. Sometimes I called him sergeant. He called me Blue 'cause of my clothes.

Don't you wanna go out sometime, he asked, and my mother asked, too. But by then I had a good path through my house, and as long as everyone kept it clear, I was fine. What was I going to do, go out and see the world? Besides, I'm allergic to dogs. (*They make seeing-eye ponies, too. Supposed to live longer.*) I was fine at home, I said. It was easier. ▶

> ❝ At night, he'd play video games. . . . Sometimes we played two-player. I'd shoot randomly or push buttons when he told me to. ❞

"Blind" *(continued)*

He mowed the lawn. He bought groceries. He turned nineteen inside me. I'd listen to the sounds he and his friends made. Sometimes they left on a movie or a game, and the TV would play the same minute-long soundtrack over and over. After it stopped being annoying, it became relaxing.

It's easier to relax when you're blind. To sit still. I could spend an entire afternoon lying on the sofa half-listening to music. Or sitting in the bathtub, warming up the water and adding multilevel-marketing-brand bath foam. One day he came home with furry handcuffs and hooked me to the headboard while he went out to deliver subs. I didn't mean to, but I fell asleep before he came home for dinner.

The pizza-and-subs delivery boy was a good cook. I could lose whole hours thinking about what he might be buying at the grocery store. Or what sounds he might bring home. The zap-ping of a BB gun shooting cans outside? The growl of car races? Digital explosions that sometimes sound real? And would he touch me during or before or after? I could lose whole hours thinking about that.

He joined the army at some point. I'm not sure when. We'd joked about it, but I guess somewhere along the way he decided to do it, 'cause eventually he had to go away. I was sad, but he promised to have his friends check up on me—the one with the ponytail and the one with the deep voice. They came most afternoons, and sometimes in the evenings, too. I think it was afternoons and evenings; they blend together. The one with the ponytail would take care of the lawn, and the one with the deep voice would keep my path clear and make sure I had groceries. The one with the ponytail had a long scar running

> " He joined the army at some point. . . . I was sad, but he promised to have his friends check up on me—the one with the ponytail and the one with the deep voice. "

14

down the side of his leg. Sometimes I'd have sex with both of them at the same time.

I missed a lot of phone calls. Most calls. I wouldn't notice them, or the guys would tell me my cell phone was blinking and I'd forget to check. I'd just lose track—couldn't very well leave myself a note on the refrigerator. One day, my mother stopped in. She was angry and said the kitchen was a mess and that there were team posters and beer signs hanging all over the living room. I didn't know, *but I don't mind*, I said. She said I should get a job, and wasn't I worried, and what was I doing with my life. She said she was sick and getting old, and that if I'd paid any attention, I'd have noticed. *Blind*, I had to remind her. *In my head, you look fine—and you finally got your ears pierced after all these years.* She laughed at the time, but still she died a little while later. I didn't see it coming. The guys said I was better off skipping the funeral. Not a good time to go out, they said.

The one with the deep voice wanted to join the army, and the one with the ponytail said he was in already, but I wasn't sure 'cause of the ponytail. They had a lot of friends with short haircuts though. They'd come over and eat pizza and call me Blue. They felt bad for me 'cause of my mother and plus the whole blind thing. They took care of the cooking and talked about the war and gave me beer and played video games and shot BB guns out back all night long. Nights I was alone, I couldn't sleep without leaving some noise on in the background. The one who cried sometimes helped me find the right button on the game machine.

They always left the path clear, the guys. That was a house rule they all maintained. Even after I lost track of them—the one ▶

> 66 When I followed the path to the bedroom and crawled into bed, I never knew who'd be there. Sleeping. Or resting or flipping through a magazine. It was like being at a slumber party or having a lot of really big cats. 99

"Blind" *(continued)*

with the dimple and the really tall one and the one who used to have a ponytail and the ones who walked around with no shirts on. The pizza-and-subs delivery boy came back for a visit once, but I lost track of him, too. His stomach was harder, his earrings were gone, and he said *Yeah, boy* a lot. When I followed the path to the bedroom and crawled into bed, I never knew who'd be there. Sleeping. Or resting or flipping through a magazine. It was like being at a slumber party or having a lot of really big cats. Except sometimes, I'd hide under the bed and wait for one of the ones with no shirt on to find me and tickle me and take me from behind.

Most of the guys left at the same time. They said they'd be back soon. (*Before you know it, Blue.*) The one who cried sometimes and one I didn't know much were the last to go, and I haven't seen them in a few weeks. They left my path clear, though, and gave me all sorts of creative foods: dehydrated something and protein-rich something else. And they'll be back soon. At night—at least I think it's night—I'll sit in my bubble bath and listen for them (zap-ping, *Yeah, boy*) outside my window. And when I'm falling asleep, I'll play the digital explosions from the game box, and I'll imagine that I'm the girl in the video game waiting to be rescued. ◄